BIG JIM

GWENDOLYN "G.C." CARTER

Copyright © 2025 Gwendolyn "G.C." Carter.

All rights reserved. No part of this book may be reproduced, stored, or transmitted by any means—whether auditory, graphic, mechanical, or electronic—without written permission of both publisher and author, except in the case of brief excerpts used in critical articles and reviews. Unauthorized reproduction of any part of this work is illegal and is punishable by law.

ISBN: 979-8-89419-593-3 (sc)
ISBN: 979-8-89419-594-0 (hc)
ISBN: 979-8-89419-595-7 (e)

Because of the dynamic nature of the Internet, any web addresses or links contained in this book may have changed since publication and may no longer be valid. The views expressed in this work are solely those of the author and do not necessarily reflect the views of the publisher, and the publisher hereby disclaims any responsibility for them.

One Galleria Blvd., Suite 1900, Metairie, LA 70001
(504) 702-6708

DEDICATION

Big Jim is dedicated especially to readers that like to read everything; everything but the bible, that is. It's not meant to take away from the bible or to indicate that God's word is a joke, it's not. Please don't ever take His word lightly!

What God has led me to do is to take a famous character of the bible, Goliath, and bring a story to life that hopefully will inspire you to actually read the bible itself. It's much more interesting than you think!

ACKNOWLEDGEMENTS

Above all, I must honor God the Father, God the Son and God the Holy Spirit, for the three are One. I gladly ab freely acknowledge that the creativity of this book is inspired by the Holy Spirit, and I am so grateful that He has seen firt to guide me in every book I have had the privilege to write; especially "Big Jim". Between researching various things and "wisdom nuggets" being downloaded into me, I have learne so much about myself, about the bible and about God Himself and what can and will happen when we open ourselves up to be used by Him.

And I want to thank everyone (too many to name), that have prayed me through this process. Thank you all for being there, helping me in your own special way. My constant prayer is that God will reward you bountifully for everything you did for me, everything that You gave me and poured into me.

INTRODUCTION

Big Jim is just that, BIG. He is seven feet, six inches tall and his weight is in the neighborhood of four hundred pounds. His shoe size is eighteen wide. For as long as he can remember, his size has either intimidated people or made some guys provoke fights with him. He hated violence, but when he did have to fight, it didn't bode well for his enemy, as he was also quick, strong and powerful. Knowing this bout himself, he tried extremely hard to not lose his temper. This was one of the reasons he was pretty much a loner Jim was a kind and gentle man and would do anything he could to help a person in need. His best and only friend Gwennie, called him a giant teddy bear, which always made him laugh. In all the years they had known one another, (That had been fifteen years now), she had never seemed to care about his size. She had always been a true, kind and gentle friend to him. He could talk to him about anything. And even when he felt down, she always knew how to make him feel better and even make him laugh, sometimes until he cried. She was the one person he always knew he could trust, and he deeply valued their friendship, and there was nothing he wouldn't do for his best friend. One of the things that made their friendship so special was that they were so different. He was a tall and big brown skinned Caucasian biker type, and always dressed as such. He had long salt and pepper hair and tattoos up and down his arms. Gwennie on the other hand, was five feet, four inches tall and was a full-figured lady. She was always neatly and comfortably dressed and upon appearance, there was nothing that would make you think that these two were the best of friends, and yet, they were. And Big Jim liked that just fine. There was nothing he wouldn't do for his Gwennie, and he knew there was nothing she wouldn't do for him. Until Gwennie, Jim lived a life of solitude for so long that he really didn't even think about it. He just went on with life, doing what he had to do and enjoying his bikes. But when he met Gwennie ad they had become friends, he began to realize just how alone he had been in this world. And he'd been in this world a long time. Gwennie had once asked him his age and he had almost told her but thought better of it. He thought that either she wouldn't believe him, or she would end their friendship if she did believe him. And that he didn't think he could bear. After being alone for so long, his life finally had vibrancy. He felt more alive than he had felt in a long time. He no longer felt like a misfit, Gwennie made him feel like he belonged. He felt that he belonged to her and to their friendship if nothing else. And frankly, he didn't feel that he needed to belong to anyone else. He loves his friend Gwennie and he knew she oved him.

CHAPTER ONE

James Wilson Beardsley loved the open road and his bike. So, on this beautiful, sunny Saturday, he decided to hit the road to wherever he ended up. He had called his best friend, Gwennie, to see if she would like to ride with him, but she was busy with housework and later had some plans to go out with other friends. He was a little disappointed and even a little jealous, but not surprised. He knew she had other friends and they all oved her dearly, just as she loved them. Still, he thought it would have been nice to have her riding with him. In all the years they'd been friends, she had only ridden with him three times. He'd known it wasn't among her favorite things to do, but she had still made the best of it each time. There had been lots of laughter, as they would stop along the way to eat and enjoy the sights. Yes, he had hoped to have her along with him, but he knew he culdn't be selfish, no matter how much he wanted to be. He had a few acquaintances that enjoyed biking as much as he did. He could have called one to see if they wanted to ride for a while, but he didn't want the company of a biker buddy. He had hoped to have the company of his best friend. He thought, "Oh well. Maybe next time".

So, there he was once again alone on the open road. But it was okay. He would just cruise for a while, then maybe go back to his shop and work for a little while. He was always in his element when he was working on a bike, whether he was restoring one or building one. But even though he enjoyed his work, which was his hobby s well, he had begun to feel that there was something missing from his life. Sometimes he found himself wanting to talk to Gwennie about it, but for some reason, he could never bring himself to broach that particular subject with her, which was strange because he hd always been able to talk to her about any and everything. So why was it that he felt the way he did about this one subject. He wondered if he might actually be afraid to talk to her about the feeling that something was missing. Sand if tht was the case, why? Why was he afraid? Suddenly he felt tired and for some reason he felt old s well. He smie sadly as he thought, "Well, I am old". Indeed, Jim ws old. No one, not even Gwennie, knew his exact age. It was one of those things he could never reveal about himself. And he was so thankful that his best friend had never questioned that; she just accepted him as he was. He decided he'd ridden enough for one day. He turned back in the opposite direction of where he's been heading, thinking he would go to his shop and work for a while. But when he got there, he found that he didn't really want to do that either. In the empty shop he looked up and asked aloud, "What in the world is happening to me? Is the time close? And what of my friend, my dear Gwennie? Shouldn't she know what's to come". Suddenly he heard/thought/felt, "She knows more than you think she does. Her dreams have been revealing thins to her. The two of you are such good friends because she is a large part of what is to come. Just go home now and let yourself relx. The time is indeed close, and you will need al your strength". Without sasying a word, Jim shut the shop and headed home.

CHAPTER TWO

Gwennie was enjoying her time out with her "girls", she always did. But for some reason, she couldn't stop thinking about her dear friend, Jim. She wondered if she should have changed her plans and gone bike riding with him. He had always been such a great, undemanding and unassuming friend to her; a friend who was always there for her when she needed him to be. Yet he never asked very much of her; just took things s they were. Sure, once in a while he would ask that she go bike riding, which she really didn't ike, but when he asked, she always sensed tht he needed her with him for some reason. He'd even bought her the riding gear—pants, boots, jacket and helmet. He had given that to her some years ago as a Christmas present. She smiled as she thought about that. "Who, Gwennie, you want to come back to earth? We're waiting for you to order here", her friend Lynn said. Gwennie gave herself a mental shake and said, "Oh, I'm so sorry", and proceeded to give the waitress her order. "Okay, so girl, where is your mind? It's like you suddenly checked out on us", Delia said with a chuckle. "Oh, I don't know. For soe reason Ican't get Jim off my mind. He wanted me to ride with him today, but I didn't because I needed to finish my housework and I didn't want to cancel my plans with you crazy ladies". Delia asked, "What is is about that guy. I mean, I know the two of you are good friends and all, but something about him scares me. Don't ask me why. What few tiemes I have been around him, he's been very sweet and respectful, not at all what you would expect when you just see him. And I think we all know that that man loves his dear friend Gwennie. And you know what? In all these years, I have never heard you say how you two met". Gwennie laughed as she remembered her first encounter with Big Jim". As they sat waiting for their food, she began to tell them about that first meeting.

CHAPTER THREE

It hd been fifteen years since she had first met James "Jim" Beardsley. After working on her new book all day, Gwennie decided to get out of the house for a while. She didn't want to cook so she decided to go to her Ted and Winnie's Café. They were friends of her's, so she liked to frequent their business. Besides, friends or not, their food was always hot and good, and everything was always so clean. She went in and saw that her favorite table was available, so she quickly went over and sat down. "Ted came over and said enthusiastically, "Well here's our Gwennie. We wondered when we would see you again. It has been a few weeks you know". They both laughed and Gwennie said, "I went back home for a couple of weeks and since I've been back I've been busy working. Those books don't write themselves, you know". They both laughed. "So how was everything back in, what is it, "Rock Run"? Yep, that's where I grew up. Actually, it's Fieldale, Virginia, but Rock Run is the community I grew up in. And everything there is good, thanks. I have an aunt who jkust celebrated her eightieth birthday, so it was great to see her". "Oh wow, that sounds good. Well, it's good to have you back ere with us. Now what can I get for you"? She gave Ted her order for hamburger steak, mashed potatoes, brussel sprouts and iced tea. As she waited for her food, she had taken out her notebook she kept with her and began to jot down notes for her book. As she did so, the tallest man she had ever seen walked through the door of the café. She wasn't normally one to judge, but for some reason she saw the long hair, tattoos and biker garb and assumed he was nothing but trouble. His size certainly didn't help. To her, he looked lik a small mountain walking through that door. As a matter of fact, he's had to stoop a bit to fit though the door. And when he had spoken to Ted, his voice had actually sounded like thunder to her. Okay, maybe that had been an exaggeration, but he had a deep distinct voice that commanded attention, whether he wanted it or not. As he sat at the counter, she heard him, and Ted begin to talk about some bike he was building. Oh well, that was their conversation, not her's, so she went back to jotting down her notes. Suddenly there were screams from other customers and when Gwennie looked up she sw two men waving guns about and demanding money nd jewelry. With a quickness James "Jim" Beardsley laid that noise o rest. It was amazing to see such a big man move with such quickness. In fact his movements seemed to be a blur as he took the pistols from both robbers simultaneously, picked them both up by their collars and put them out of the café. By the time the police arrived, the culprits were glad to get out of the presence of the giant that had foiled their robbery attempt. Gwennie hadn't even been aware that she had been feverishly taking notes the whole time, until Ji had come to her table and asked, "Ma'a, are you alright? It seems you are because I know you have been writing this whole time. If I may ask, are you a reporter"? "Oh no. I'm an author. Hey, that was amazing. You're built like a mountain and yet you moved so quickly that it all seemed ike a blur". Then she thought she might have offended him when she said he was built like a mountain. "Oh, you know what? I'm so sorry about the mountain thing. I shouldn't have said that". It was then that he began to laugh with that thunderous voice of his, and the laugh was infectious. She couldn't help but laugh with him. Once the laughter had stopped, they had introduced themselves to one another and that had been the beginning of one of the unlikeliest friendships. By the time she had finished sharing that memory with her friends, they were hallway finished with their food. After a brief silence, Delia said, "Wow. That was some meeting. If I had been there, I think I would have wanted him as my friend too". They all laughed and talked about current events in each of their lives. They all laughed a lot, but Gwennie still couldn't stop thinking about her friend, her "Big Jim". She decided she would call him when she got home as long as it wasn't too late. She knew she was free to call him any time of day or night, just as he was with her. But they respected each other and their friendship and only used that privilege when absolutely necessary. With her mind made up, she focused on the present company she was with

CHAPTER FOUR

Jim answered on the first. He'd had a feeling that Gwennie would call when she got home. He thought it was so funny how the two of them just knew things like that about one another. Like when one of them really needed one another. They just seemed to know somehow, or rather feel the other one's need. "Hi Gwennie. Did you have fun with your friends"? "I did, but you kept staying on my mind. What's up with you my friend"? "Oh, nothing for you to worry your pretty little head about". "Hoping sweet talk can change the subject, are we"? He had known it wouldn't work but thought he would try it anyway. "I don't know what's going on. I think I'm just feeling tired. And old. Tired and old, that's quite a combination, isn't it", he asked in an attempt at humor. They laughed and she said, "Well, you are old, my friend. Not quite old as dirt, but getting there", she said as she laughed. And he said, "Hey, don't forget, you are not far behind". They went back and forth on the age thing for a couple of minutes, laughing and teasing one another. But in the back of

BIG JIM

his mind, he kept thinking, "You have no idea of just how close to the truth you are, my friend. Then he found himself wondering what she would do if he really did know his true age. Would she freak out? Would she even believe him? Would she choose to end their friendship? Then he thought, "No. This is Gwennie. Maybe he would be shocked, but she would just accept it and roll with it. He had no doubt that. "Hey, you got quiet on me. What's going on with you Jim? And I want the truth". "Gwennie, I don't know. It just feels like something is happening or going to happen". He heard her sharp intake of breath and remembered what he had heard earlier in the shop. She had been having dreams. "Gwennie, now it's my turn to ask you if you are alright". "Oh, I'm okay. That statement just kind of threw me for a minute, that's all". She wondered if she should mention the dreams she had been having, and decided against it, at least for that present moment. "Anyway, you do still know that I'm here and you can talk to me anytime, about anything you need to talk about, right"? "I do know that my Gwennie. And you know the same applies for you, right"? "Of course. You have proven to be the best friend anyone could hve or even hope to have, my mountain of a friend". At that they both howled with laughter as they remembered how they first met. And after they had each shared a few details about their evenings, they had prayer together and said good night. After ending the call Jim said "Thank You Lord for my friend and for sending her into this thing with me. Somehow, I feel better, stronger, knowing we will be in this thing together. Just please help me to watch over her as You watch over us both". A sense of peace enveloped him as he drifted off to sleep. Gwennie on the other hand was wide awake. She couldn't shake the feeling that something heavy was on the mind of her friend. And she now, after his comment about something coming, she sensed that whatever he felt was coming was connected t the dreams she had been having. She had been having those dreams, almost futuristic in nature, for about seven months now. When they first started, she thought it was the start of new book, although it didn't seem to be like any other book she had written. And every one of those dreams seemed more like reality than dreams. And Jim was always in those dreams with her. When she would wake up, she would expect herself to be in the last location of her most recent dream. She would have to sit in bed and get her bearings before she would realize that she was back to real ife instead of in a dream. Even as a small child, she had learned that many of her dreams had meanings to them and she knew these dreams were of that nature. As her friend had said, something was either happening or was going to happen. Either way, she was truly grateful to have Jim in it with her. She knew he wasn't God or anything like that but remembering how he had handled those robbers at Ted and Winnie's Café made her feel much better about dealing with whatever was coming. She finally felt sleep overtaking her and was in one of those dreams.

The landscape had obviously been ravaged by time and war. The world was all but colorless. She was walking through what she assumed must have been a town once upon a time. And as usual, she was dressed in clothes the likes of which she had never seen, and she was carrying in her right hand a very shiny golden sword. Even though some details of the dreams changed, those two details remained the same. Suddenly she heard Jim calling her. "Gwennie. Gwennie, where are you"? I'm over here, Jim. Over by the old well". He soon turned the corner and saw her standing there. "Well, I haven't seen another living soul. How about you"? "No one. It's as though everyone has just vanished from the face of the earth. Well, everyone but the two of us, that is". "Yes. That's how it appears to be", he said pointedly. "You think someone is hiding from us"? "Someone or something". She knew what he meant and sid nothing else. They walked the dusty road together in silence for a while. All of a sudden, they heard a strange howling, growling and gurgling sound coming from one single source that was behind them and they turned to see what the source of that sound was, swords in ready position. But when they turned, they nothing and no one, yet the sound continued, as though it was beckoning thm to come back to where it was. They looked at each other and without speaking a word agreed that it was only a distraction, meant to deter them from going forward to do what they knew they were destined to do. As soon as they faced forward again the strange sound stopped. "Jim, wasn't that strange? I mean, the way those three sounds came from the same source at the same time". "It's a strange sound every time, my Gwennie", he said looking at her pointedly. She looked up at him with a puzzled look and asked, "You've heard tha sound before"? "Yes, my friend. And so have you. You just don't remember hearing it". And that's when Gwennie was awakened back into reality. And once again it took her a couple of minutes to realize that she was no longer in her dream state, but in real life. Once she had come to that realization, she said to an empty bedroom, "Okay, Jim and I have got to talk. What does that mean? Have I heard that sound before, in real life I mean? I don't remember even hearing that sound in any dream before, much less in real life. Jim knows something. Much more than he is telling. And I need to know what it is that he knows and how it applies to me and my life". She looked at her bedside clock and saw that it was only four forty-three in the morning. She knew she wouldn't be able to go back to sleep, so she thought she would wash her face, make some coffee and begin her morning devotion. And oh boy, did she ever need that communication with her Savior, Jesus Christ. She needed some answers and she felt that she needed them sooner than yesterday.

CHAPTR FIVE

By the time his alarm went off at seven thirty, Jim had already been up for hours. He had fallen asleep in his recliner, but that had only been for about two hours. He had gotten up and prepared himself for bed, but by the time he climbed between the sheets he was wide awake. When he looked at his bedside clock, he saw that it was just past midnight. Wow. He thought he'd slept longer than that. He thought about Gwennnie and hoped she was sleeping well. Without stopping to think about it, he said, "Lord, if she's not sleeping well, please change that. You said she's having dreams. Please don't let them be too bad, okay"? He went back into the den and sat in his recliner again nd thought about Gwennie. Gwennie. His best friend Gwennie. His Gwennie. She ws the one and only person in the whole world that he could say he loved beyond the depths of his heart and soul. He loved people in general and would do whatever he could to help a soul in trouble. But his Gwennie had a special place in his heart that no one hd ever occupied nor would anyone else ever occupy it. Only his Gwennie had taken a seat in that place, and it seemed that without trying to, she had closed the door and locked herelf in. But Jim didn't mind. He didn't mind at all. He thought about their first meeting. There were some people that could have called him a mountain and he wouldn't have liked it. But with Gwennie, he lovfed it. It had made him feel special somehow. And when he heard her laugh, that was it for him. That sweet and infectious laughter had captured his heart. He loved her honesty as she told him how she had judged him upon first sight and had then apologized to him. She had even told him that he had taught her a valuable lesson on judgementalism. And he had admitted that when he first saw her, he knew he wanted to get to know her. What he had never admitted, even after all the years they'd been friends, was that his very first thought was that he wanted to marry her. That had shocked him because in all the years of his life, and there were many of them, he had never seen anyone he thought he would like to be marrie to. Over the years he hd finally admitted to himself that he not only loved her, but that he was in love with her. But marriage was not an option for them. There were just too many reasons for it not working, starting with the age difference. That alone would be a huge problem, even if she did believe him and accept it. And there were other reasons as well. He felt that a certain level of intimacy would be completely out of the question. That would be like putting a walking mountain with a baby doll, which was how he felt when they were out together. Sometimes he wondered if people that saw them together from any distance wondered if he was a father with his small child. He always chuckled at that thought. If she knew about it, she would laugh outright. "Anyway", he thought, "Marriage has always been and always will be out of the question, so I am grateful for the friendship we have. And in a way, it is like a sort of marriage, I think. The friendship we share is a form of commitment between us and I know nothing nd no one can break it. So, I'm as satisfied as I can be, and I thank You for that much Lord". He thought it ws likely tht he wouldn't be going back to sleep so got up to put o n a pot of coffee and then searched for a good program to watch on television. He finally found an old movie to watch. I" I Am Gabriel" would always be a favorite of his. He loved the way it depicted the various ways people can react when God is working right before their eyes. With the coffee done brewing, he made himself a cup and settled himself back in his recliner to enjoy the movie. But halfway through it, he brgsn to feel a familiar but odd sensation course through his body. It was like a surge of electricity that was changing things in him as it made its way through him. It had been fifteen years since he's felt that, but he knew all too well what it meant. When he had felt it fifteen years ago, two robbers had come into Ted and Winnie's Café and attempted to commit a robbery. But following a "leading" from within, Jim had known that he had to be there and what he's had to do. And later as he and Gwennie began the beginning of their friendship, he had known that although there had been others in the Café that were protected, Gwennie was the main reason he'd had to be there. He'd had to be in position to protect his best friend, whom he loved more than life itself. Without another thought, he got dressed, got on his bike and headed west. Two miles later he saw a car approaching at sucvh a high rate of speed that it had begun to hydroplane. Not stopping to think of what he was doing, Jim got off his bike and just as the car was about to hit a telephone pole, he caught it and set it down gently. As he went to walk away the driver, who'd been very drunk prior to that incident, began to question whether he had just seen what had just happened. And who, or what was that that had caught his car in midair and set it down? It looked like a really huge man, but were there any men that big? Had he just seen a Sasquatch? Nah. That had to be an angel. Yeah. That's what it had to be. He had just seen an angel. Had to be. Either way he sure was glad because he knew that he and his passengers should have been dead or at the very least, hurt badly in what would have been a very bad accident. The driver looked around to thank who ever had helped them, but he saw no one. He looked in every direction, and no matter which way he looked, he should have seen someone, some movement. But he saw absolutely no one. He said aloud, more to convince himself thn his passengers,

"Yeah Man. That had to be an angel". He made up his mind right then and there that he's had his last drink and smoked his lst blunt. Three years later, that same young man became an ordained minister and still told the story of that night to anyone who would listen.

Back at home, Jim washed his face and hands, warmed the coffee and sat down to have a cup before starting g his day. "Lord, I know that with You, so many hinges onposition and timing. Thank You for leading me to that spot at just the right time. I just hope those young men know that it's Your grace and mercy that has kept them alive". Jim had been used in many instances in which lives had been saved, but he didn't always have that strange sensation that would lead him to certain places at certain times. He had tried to figure that out many times over his man years on earth, had even sked about it. But since he'd never gotten an answer, he figured that was just the good Lord's way of saying that it was none of his business. He looked at the clock on the wall. Seven eighteen. He wondered if Gwennie was up yet, then thought he would just wait to call her. He enjoyed starting his day with a conversation with his best friend. That seemed to bring a joy into his day that nothing could take away. Once again, he thanked God for his precious friend.

CHAPTER SIX

Gwennie, having finished with her morning devotion, showered and dressed for the day. She went into the kitchen to start her coffee and figure out what she wanted for breakfast. She decided she would have two hard boiled eggs, toast with grape jelly and her cup of coffee. That would hold her for a while, long enough to get four or five chapters done anyway. She thought about Jim and figured he was probably already at his bike shop. And as if he had somehow reah her mind, her phone rang, and it was him caslling. "Okay, I have told you before to stop reading my mind like that". They both laughed. That was his Gwennie alright, starting the day out with laughter. They talked for a little while and ended with him telling her that "It" had happened again; how he had been directed to the sight of what would have been a horrible accident. "My friend, I have told you before. I still believe that you are some kind of an angel. I just don't believe human being could do the things you do, and especially with the se speed with which you do them. You are an angel. That's my story and I'm not changing it without proof that I am wrong. There. Case closed on that". They both laughed again, prayed and wished each other a great day. After the morning call was over and as Gwennie was having her breakfast, Jim thought, for what must have been the millionth time, about Gwennie's surety that he was an angel. She wasn't th only one to make that statement. Others he had been sent to help had called him an angel too. The way he saw it, he was just someone being used to give others a helping hand. All he ever needed anyone to know, if they needed to know, was that he was James "Jim" Beardsley, servant of the Lord Most High.

Gwennie was now over an hour into her new book, "Please Don"t Pass the Sugar", a comical novel regaling stories from her teen to young adult years. As she wrote she thought about Jim. It was nothing strange for him to call and tell her that he had helped someone in danger. He never bragged about it; it was just his way of testifying about the goodness of the Lord. He was aways so humble in the telling of these incidences. There would be something like a childlike innocence when he shared these things with her. And it always touched her heart. Most people probably would want to have things like that in the newspaper and on the CBS evening news, or at least have it reported on the local news. But not her dear friend Jim. That mountain of a man had a heart that seemed to be almost as big as he was. She had seen some of the things he had done, especially when he hd foiled the robbery at the café. She had seen him feed the hungry, put homeless people in motel rooms when it was cold especially. He did that for a few men, but he mostly did it for women, especially when they had children n the streets with them. She had also seen him run and play with kids in the park. The kids loved playing with him, but the parents were usually afraid of him and would call the kids over to them. Every time that happened, she could see the hurt in his eyes. She would hyrt with him, but mostly she really wanted to explain to the parents that their kids couldn't be in safer hands, and that they shouldn't judge him or anyone else for any reason. But he never wanted her to say anything, so she never did. Once again, she found herself wondering why he had never been married. She had once asked him about that and his answer had been, "Aww, who'd want to marry me? I'm not a handsome man, I'm not rich by the world's standards, I'm so big I'm like a walking mountain to most people, especially to a certain woman (he'd laughed at that), and well, I'm just too old". Even then he hadn't said how old he was. But she always felt that if he had given himself the chance, he would have been a great husband and even a great father. But that wasn't any of her business. What mattered was that he had been a great friend to her for fifteen years. He had always been honest, loyal, understanding and he was very protective of her. She loved her dear friend, and she knew he loved her. He showed it in so many ways.

For instance, for fifteen years she had always gotten that morning call to check on her and pray with her and the night calls to see if everything was okay, pray with her and say good night. And when she needed him for anything it was like he somehow instinctively knew it. He would either call or show up. Yes, James "Jim" Beardsley was indeed a special man and friend. And she never wanted to lose the friendship they shared.

CHAPTER SEVEN

"Hey Jim, your girlfriend just drove up", yelled one of Jim's two employees, Mike Siegley. He always called Gwennie Jim's girlfriend. "Tell her to come on in the office", and when he looked up, she was standing at eh door. "Hey my Gwennie. What's the reason for this pleasant surprise"? "Oh, so now I need a reason to surprise you", she asked and laughed. "Oh no. You know you don't ever need a reason to come here. But are you okay though"? "Well, there is one thing wrong". He looked at her with concern and solemnly asked, "What is it Gwenie? What's wrong"? She couldn't keep herself from laughing, and said, I'm like super hungry and I want to have lunch with my friend. My treat this time. How about it"? "Sounds goo except for one thing. This gentleman always pays. So. Where do you want to go, dear lady"? "Well, since Ted and Winnie's café is right next door, why not eat there? I'm hungry for their meatloaf today". "Mumm. That sounds good. I just might have that myself. Let me get washed up and we'll go, okay"? "Sounds good".

Big Jim

From behind the counter, Ted and Winnie were watching their friends as the two were enjoying their lunch and each other. They both had seen long ago that Jim and Gwennie had a special relationship, a special for one another. Winnie was once again wondering why the two of them hadn't gotten married. Since the death of her husband at a young age, Gwennie just never seemed to be interested in anyone else. Well, no one else but Big Jim. And his shop had been right next door to the café since they'd been there, so he had eaten there quite often. But Gwennie was the only woman he had ever eaten there with. She knew that he obviously had a life she didn't know bout and could have dated other women, but she had a strong suspicion that wasn't the case at all. To Winnie, there was just something about the way Jim had changed once he and Gwennie had become friends. He laughed a whole lot more. And the way he looked at "his Gwennie" and the way he talked to her, well, if Jim had ever had another woman in his life that of course was his business. But to Winnie, it was obvious that Gwennie had that big heart of his in the palm of his in her hands, something Winnie still believed had ever happened for Big Jim Beardsley. Winnie smiled as their joy together brought her heart gret joy. She was crazy about them both and wanted them happy, whether together or apart. In her heart, she knew that it would e together for he two of them. "What are you smiling about, Win"? Ted already knew the answer, as he had been watching their friends as well. He knew what his wife was thinking. He kissed her forehead and said, "Maybe one day Win. Maybe one day". Just then some customers came in so they both got busy, each still thinking about Jim and Gwennie.

Gwennie and Jim had never even noticed that Ted and Winnie were watching them. They were in their own world, deep in conversation. They had carried on their usual banter until their food has arrived and grace had been said. Then as they began to enjoy their meals, the serious talk had begun. "Jim, I need to talk to you about something. And just as importantly, I need you to really talk to me. It's really important to me, and well, I think to you as well. It's something you said that started me to thinking". Seeing the concern on his friend's face, added to hearing it in her voice gripped Jim's heart. He hated seeing her that way, but he knew what she wanted to talk about and he knew that the time had come to have that conversation. He also knew that it was no coincidence that they were seated in a semi=secluded area of the café. With no one sitting too closely to them, they could talk freely, at least until the café filled up, which he knew It would do. The food was really good, and Ted and Winnie made everyone feel welcome.

"Okay, my Gwennie. No one's around so wecan talk about this". "I should have known you would already know what's on my mind. So, do anges read minds too"? She smiled as she asked the question.

"Well, you'll have to ask an angel about that". "I already am". Then the conversation began in earnest. "Do you remember saying that something was either happening or that something was coming"? With a sight he said, "Yeah. I do remember saying that. Gwennie, is this about the dreams you've been having"? She gave him a startled look and finally said, "I don't know why I am always so surprised that you know things like that. But yes, I almost began telling you about the dreams when you said that. She began to tell him about the dreams; how no matter what else changed in them, the two of them always wore the same clothes and thy always had those shiny golden swoirds in their right hands. And even though she knew they were always in different "towns", each one looked the same—dry, colorless, dusty and empty. They always had the look of almost apocalyptic destruction. Then she began to tell him of that strange howling, gurgling and growling sound that they both had heard that had come from the same source, all at the same time. She told him that they had raised their swords and had been battle ready, but when they turned around, they saw nothing and no one. She finished by telling him that in he dreams he had told her that they had both heard that sound before and that it was a distraction meant to stop them from going where they had to go and doing what they had to do. It was then that a measure of surprise and concern had registered on Jim's face. "Jim, what Is it? Why are you looking like that"? "Not here, Gwennie.

Not here and ot now". She both knew and trusted him well enough to accept that. So, the conversation was over as well s their meal. Jim paid the ticket and they left. Neither Ted nor Winnie missed the solemn looks on their friends' faces, but neither of them said anything about it. When they were alone though, they both wondered what cvould have happened to cause such sa change iin Gwennie and Jim. They both knew it had to be something quite serious. "Well Winnie, I guess it's just not our business to know what's going on. But that's one friendship I really hope never breaks up. I've never seen two happier people than when those two are together.

Once they were outside Jim asked Gwennie If she could come into shop for a little while. Once they were in his office and the door was closed, he asked her a question that her mind didn't need asking. "Gwennie, do you trust me? I mean, really trust me"? "Jim, you already know…". He interrupted her and said, "No, Gwennie. Do you have what I would call a life-or-death trust? If it came to it, would you trust me with your life? Right now, that's the main question I need you to answer before our conversation can go any further. So. Do you trust me with your life"? "Jim, have you forgotten how we met? Had you not been there and done what you did, I could have died that day, along with other people. And for over fifteen years now you have always been right where I need you to be, when I need you to be there. You have proven to be a true and valuable friend, so yes, I have to say I would trust you with my life. I mean we both know God has total control of life and death, but I trust you to do what you can to protect me. Now, please tell me what thi is about, okay"? "I will, my Gwennie, a little at a time. With each lesson I will tell you more". "Whoa. Lessons. What lessons? What in the world are we talking about here"? "There are things I need to teach you to prepare you for what's coming. The lessons won't be easy, but they will be quite effective. And we need to start as soon as possible". "Why am I just hearing about these lessons? What am I about to start learning"? "I've said as much as I can for right now, my Gwennie. Soon, you will know more than you want to. Much more". With a puzzled and frightened look Gwennie said, "Okay Jim. Whatever you say". They tried to converse about other, lighter things, but it just didn't come easy that time. So Gwennie said she thought she'd better get home and go to work on her book. Jim usually asked questions about her books, but not this time. He had his mind on other, more solemn things.

Back at home, Gwennie sat at her computer and tried to write, but it just wasn't happening. There was no flow at all. It was as if the "word river" had dried up. Sometimes when the words did not come, she would play a game so she tried that, but she couldn't concentrate on it. She loved Solitaire, but she couldn't concentrate on it, so she just turned the computer off. She decided se would walk the trail that was behind her house and commune with the Lord. That was something that usually mde her feel better. She put on her hiking boots and grabbed her walking stick and was on her way. As she walked, she truly did commune with God, asking Him more questions than she'd initially realized she wanted to ask. And one question was just what kind of lessons Jim need oto teach her. Would it be martial arts? Or something like fencing, since in he dreams, she and Jim always had those golden swords in their hands. What other kind of lessons could there be for her t learn? Then she heard/felt, "You must teach your heart to listen". "Huh? Teach my heart to listen? What does that mean"? She thought it might mean to see people for their heart, not physical attributes. But that would be seeing though. "Okay, I need some clarity on that. What does it mean to teach to teach your heart to listen? And how do you do that"? Then she heard clearly, "Sit down on that stum up on your right. Once she hd done so, she heard, "Shhh. Be still and be quiet. Not only you, Gwennie, but so many people need to learn to be silent in mouth and mind. Now, stop trying to figure this out. Concentrate on the stillness here. The silence. Focus on that. Take deep breaths and release them slowly and just focus on the quiet. She did her best to follow directions, but her mind was still on so many things. She still thought about her conversation with Jim. She thought about how she could work what she ws experiencing into a new book. And she thought about trying to be still and silent. The still part she had gotten, she hadn't moved at all. And even though she was quiet with her mouth, her mind refused to cooperate. Her mind had a mind of its own. (She giggled at that thought). She cleared her throat, wiggled the slightest bit on the stump, then tried even harder to concentrate on the silence of the wooded trail. After a while, she didn't know how long, she felt an unfamiliar calmness envelope her. She knew calm, but this was beyond what one would consider to be the "norml" kind of calm. This calmness not only enveloped her, but it seemed to hone her senses somehow, or was that her imagination? She didn't know for sure. All she knew was that she was experiencing something new, and kind of exciting. When she was free to walk back to her house, she thought she just couldn't wait to tell Jim about it. She didn't think anyone else would understand, but she knew for a fact that Jim would. She wondered if the lessons ha already begun, even though he wasn't anywhere around.

Jim spent as much of the afternoon, as he possibly could, in his office. He needed to think, and this wasn't the kind of thinking he would be able to do while carrying on conversations with anyone. Gwennie knew nothing of the "old ways", and he needed to hear clearly to know how to go about teaching her what she needed to know. She would definitely need strength training, for the swords were heavy. She had seen them in her dreams but wouldn't have any idea of just how big and how heavy they were. Each blade was two feet long from tip to guard. The knuckle guard was another six inches. And on top of the pommel was a six-inch cross which, until you learned how to hold and handle the sword, made it difficult to work with. The entire sword from blade tip to the tip of the cross was three feet long with the cross on it, and it weighed ten pounds. To him that was nothing, but then he was used to it. Gwennie, however, was on five feet, four inches tall, and while liting a ten-pound bag of potatoes was light work to her, she had never had to carry a sword like that. And she certainly hadn't ever had to fight using oe. But one thing he knew about his Gwennie was that she was a quick learner. He also knew she was inquisitive and determined enough to want to learn all there was to learn. She would do well. The physical aspects of her training would be a little rough in the beginning, but she was one tough lady. She come through with shining colors.

After a long hard day, Ted and Winnie were finaly settled down to relax before bedtime. Ted was trying to find a good action m,ovie to watch when Winnie said, "I can't help but wonder about Jim nd Gwennie. In all the years they have been friends, I have never seen this look so, well, miserable together. ZI know I'm being nosey, but I sure would love to know what in the world happened. I mean, they were their same old selves when they came in". "Well, Winnie, I reckon whatever happened is their business. But a couple of times I ooked over and they seemed to be deep in conversation.

I don't know, but I don't think they were arguing or anything like that. But I could tell that it was a serious conversation. I guess all we can do is pray for them and trust that everything is alright". "Yes, I guess you are right. It'd just that in all the years they have been friends, since the attempted robbery, I have never seen them like that when they are together. I don't think I have ever seen any two people have more fun together. Oh, I know we don't see them a the time. And as you said, it's none of our business, but I just can't shake the feeling that something is wrong". "Me too, Win. But like I said, all we can do is pray and do our best to be there for them if they need us. Now, I think this old horse is ready to lie down. You coming"? "I will in a few minutes Honey".

Gwennie was deep into her manuscript when the phone range. It was Delia calling to see if she could talk for a few minutes. Gwennie, hearing in her friend's voice that something was wrong yuickly said, "Sure Delia. What's up"? Delia began to tell Gwennie about the present woes of her current relationship. Gwennie didn't believe in trying to tell others how to handle their lives and relationships, listened to her friend talk. Gwennie found that usually, if you just let a person talk and from time to time ask leading questions, people will find their own answers to their problems. Gwennie had learned that when she had worked in counseling.

After getting off the phone call with Delia, Gwennie found that she was quite hungry, so she washed her hands and headed to the kitchen t make herself some dinner. She had eaten a rather heavy lunch, so she thought a chef's salad would be enough for her supper. As she gathered all the ingredients, she thought about Delia and chuckled. It seemed that poor Delia couldn't make up her mind as to whether she wanted a man in her life. The poor woman complained when there wasn't one and she complained when there was one. Gwennie had once suggested that she make two lists; one listing the positives of having a mn in her life an the other listing the negatives. Whichever list was the longest, maybe she should consider working with that. She'd said that when she tried to do that, it was of no help to her. Gwennie had a sneking suspicion that her friend had not really tried it. Maybe she had made a feeble ttempt at it, but Gwennie was almost certain that she hadn't put her heart into it, or even her mind, really.

Once her salad was made and the kitchen was all clean again, Gwennie took her salad with her, intending to eat as she worked on her book. She did get in one chapter, but beyond that she just couldn't concentrate enough to write. Her mind was going back to her conversation with Jim and then to the valuable lesson she had learned while she was on the walking trail. She once again thought she would really love to learn how to keep both her mind and her mouth silent She believed that keeping her mouth silent was less of a challenge because she spent so much of her time alone anyway. Theb she giggled, thinking, "Well, I do have my private little conversations with myself". But she figured she could silence even those conversations more easily than she could silence her mind. With being alone so much, of ourse her mind was free to roam. Especially with her being an author, where her creative mind was kept active anyway. With that thought, her mind went back to her manuscript, and that was where her mind stayed until her phone rang again. It was Jim calling to have their nightly conversation. "Oh, hello my friend. I'm so glad you called". "Oh. So, you're not gld to hear from me any other time"? That started their friendly banter back and forth. They kept the conversation light abd lkaughed a lot, but they both had more serious things on their minds. After they had finally said good night, Gwennie stomach growled in obvious anger, reminding her that she hadn't eaten any dinner. "Okay belly. I hear you. I know I've treated you badly, so et's go make up for that". She went into the kitchen, washed her hands and made herself aq BLT with cheese and grabbed a frui9t cup to go with it. She watched the news as she ate, wishing there would be a good old human-interest story on there. She very much wanted them to report some good, positive news. But it was just more o f the usual; killing, stealing, and the price of everything going up. She turned off the little television after making suer the kitchen was clean again and went back to her computer, where she worked until after midnight.

After saying goodnight to his Gwennie, Jim sat back in his trusty old recliner and reached for hi sever present cup of coffee. He wanted to find something good to watch on television, something that would take his mind off the conversation that he and Gwennie had avoided getting into on the phone. Things had been deep enough during lunch, and more of the same would have been a little too much, even for him. He had never been a man to run away from what ever had to be done, but this time it wasn;t just him. This time his dear friend Gwennie was involved so he had to make sure everything wa handled just right. He had experienced a lot of hurts in his long life and he h always been brought them, mostly unscathed. But if something were to ever happen to his Gwennie, especially if it were to be his fault, he just didn't think he coud stand that. He thought about all that he had to teach her in a relatively short time. Compared to him she wqas a little china doll, but he knew he couldn't let that stop him from giving it his all in making sure Gwennie knew all that she needed to know and ow to do what she needed to do as well as discerning the right time to get those things done. He smiled as he said to the empty room, "My Gwenny is a tough little lady. If I know her, she'll excel and start teaching me", At that thought he stared laughing. His Gwennie was quite a lady. And quite a friend. The one true friend he never, ever wanted to lose.

Ted and Winnie had been in the café since six a.m., so they heard Jim when he got to his bike shop. During the night, Ted had begun to feel that maybe it ws time to invite his friend to ride with him on Saturday so they could talk if Jim wanted to talk. Ted didn't want to apper to b nosey, but for some reason the change in both Jim and Gwennie was relly bothering him and Winnie. Those were two very sweet people that deserved to be happy, and they had always seemed to be so happy together. He knew he couldn't get involved in their relationship, that wasn't for him to do. But Ted knew he could pray and let the Lord use him, if that was meant to be. But for now, he felt like the invitation to ride was in order, and would remind his friend, Big Jim, that his old friend Ted was always there for him.

"Are you still going to see if Jim will ride wih you on Saturday"? "Yeah. I'll see if he comes in for lunch. If he doesn't, I'll walk over later and talk with him". "Okay Honey. I'm wondering if I should give Gwennie a call and see if we can get together either Friday or Sunday afternoon. I don't want to plan Saturday so you can be free to ride with Jim". "That sounds good, Win. I think that sounds really good". By this time the breakfast crown had begun to file in, so there was no time for further conversation about anything other than food orders, etc.

"Delia, I don't know if I can meet you for lunch today. I have planned to stay if front of my computer today and work on my new book". "Well, don't you have to stop to eat anyway? So, why can't we meet for a quick, well, not so quick maybe, lunch? Please Gwennie. I really do need to talk to you. This thing is driving me crazy". Gwennie looked longingly at her computer screen. She had really wanted to spend the whole day working. True, she would have stopped to eat anyway and maybe she would have stopped long enough to walk the trail behind her house. What she din't want to tell Delia was that she felt an urgency to get this book done because she knew that the lessons with Jim would have to start soon, and she needed to be able to give her full attention to that. She felt that it was just too important to not give her full attention. But she also felt that she couldn't say no to her friend Delia. They had been friends since the second grade and that was a long time. They had talked each other through some rough and hard times over the years. "Okay Delia. Where do you want to go for lunch"? "How about Cracker Barrel? I could useme some of those good old chicken livers". Gwennie laughed. "Boy are you out of touch! I love their chicken livers too, but they don't even serve those anymore". "Wow, it has been too long since I have been there. Well, do you want to go somewhere else"? "No, not really. I like Cracker Barrel's Sampler, so I guess I will have that". "Ooh, that does sound good. I think I'll have that too. So, what time are we meeting"? Gwennie looked at her watch and saw that it was nearly noon. "How about twelve thirty"? "That sounds good my dearest friend. And thank you so much. Love you". Again, Gwennie looked longingly at her computer. It wasn't as though she hadn't had her plan to change before. But she just felt such an urgency to work today. "Oh well", she thought, "my friend needs me, and I guess that's more important today". She went into hr bedroom and quickly gt dressed. She hadn't planned to fo out, so she'd been dressed in her favorite panda bear night shirt and an old pair of pajama bottoms. Now, as she headed out the door she was dressed in jeans, tshirt and tennis shoes, her second favorite attire.

Delia was waiting near the door for her when she arrived at Cracker Barrel. "Have you already been inside"? "Yeah. They'll call us in about five minutes". "Good, because with smelling all this good food, I have suddenly realized that I am absolutely starving", Gwennie said with a laugh. "So now. Aren't you glad I talked you into having lunch with me today"? They both laughed and within three minutes they were called to their table. The both ordered their Samplers and settled in to have their talk. "So, Delia. What is going on with you? I know last night you were talking about the man in your life, about your relationship. Is this a continuation of that conversation"? Slowly and thoughtfylly Delia said, "Well, yes and no. I mean, I need to talk about that, but there is something else I need to talk to you about as well". "Okay". "I just don't know where I start. I mena, so much is going on in my head. And it seems like I can't keep a complete train of thought. My mind star on track A, then jumps way over to traqck D. And girl, don't even ask me about the tracks in beteen those. I don't even get a glimpse of what may be on those tracks". She tried to laugh, but Gwennie saw that it wasn't her friend's genuine laugh. It was more of a sad, forced laugh. Having spent many years working in counseling, Gwennie's instinct told her to be silent and just let Delia talk in the way she needed to do it. In counseling you quickly learned that even though some people hoped you had the answers they needed, They often found their own answers when the had someone to just sit and listen to them as they released what was inside of them. Once in a while, they may need to be sked a guided question here and there, but very often they found their own way. And Gwennie felt certain that it would work that way with Delia.

When their food arrived, they ate quietly for a few minutes. "Um. It's not chicken livers. But it's good jst the same", Delia. "Right", Gwennie said as she put another forkful of mashed potatoes in her mouth. When they were both halfway finished eating, the conversation began in earnest. As Delia began to talk again, Gwennie reminded herelf to keep her mind and her mouth silent, as she had been directed to do while out on the wooded trail behind her house. And for the most part she was able to d just that. Twice she felt the need to ask leading questions. After talking for a while, they decided to have dessert and by the time they had finished both it and the conversation, the realized they had been sitting there for nearly two hours. They both apologixzed to the waitress for occupying the table for so long, to which the waqitress replied, "Thanks, but you are paying customers like everybody else. Besides, we're not really that crowded today". She turned to walk away, then thought better of it. She turned back, blushed and said, "Honestly Ms. Creighton, I've been hoping to get your autograph before you leave. I have my copy of ytour book, "When Water Wasn't Wet" in the back. May I please get it, and have you autograph it for me"? Gwenie was delighted and assured the waitress that she would be glad to do so. After that was done, they thanked each other and Gwennie and Delia exited the restaurant and after hugging one another went their separate ways.

It was after three p.m. and Jim was worried. Very worried. It had been hours since he had called and eft Gwennie the message tha he needed to talk to her. He knew his precious friend had other riends and a life of her own. But it wasn't like her to not return his calls as soon as she could. Now he couldn't help wondering If she ws okay. But then he thought, "She's the closest person to me, so shouldn't I know if something is wrong with her? I mean, wouldn't I have that feeling I sometimes get"? He suddenly realized that he's been thinking out loud, but it didn't apper as though any one had heard him and for that he was grateful. He decided he would call Gwenie one more itme and if he didn't get an answer he would go to her house and if he didn't find her there, he would check the trail she loved to wlk. On the third ring he heard, "Hey. I wqas just getting ready to call you. Are you okay? You sounded like something ws wrong on those last two messages". He let out a huge sigh of relief. He hadn't even realized that he's been holding his breath. "Oh, I'm good my friend. Much better now that I know you are alright". Suddenly she remembered that she had told him her plan to stay hme all day and work on her book. "Oh, I'm so sorry, Jim. I didn't mean to worry you. My plans changed. Delia really needed to talk so we met for lunch and I jkust got back home". "Hey, you don't owe me any explanations. I'm just glad you're okay"? Gwennie giggled and said, "Jim, you should be careful"? "Why is that"? Because sometimes you kind of act like a husband". He laughed at that and asked, "Does that bother you"? "Hey, you know me well enough ot know that if it bothered me, I would have told you. No, it doesn't bother me. Actually, it's nice to have a dear, dear friend to care about me like you do. Thank you". They talked a while longer, made their plans to meet he is following day and then said heir see-you-laters", knowing they would talk at least once more before bedtime.

Before he started working, he thought about Gwennie's observance of him sometimes acting like a husband. He wondered if he needed to work harder at hiding his thoughts and feelings along that line. He never wanted to make his best friend in the whole wide world uncomfortable in any way. But then again, she did say it was kind of nice to have him care about her and worry about her like that. With that thought, he decided it was time to finish the paperwork he had been trying to finish all afternoon. Now that he knew that his Gwennie was alright, he knew he ould get his work done with no problem. And there weren't any problems, but he was interrupted when Ted came in to talk to him.

"Well hey there Ted. How ya doing today"? "Hey Jim. I'm good. Things are quiet over at the café so I thought I would come ovr for a bit, see what you're working on these days". Jim knew there was more to this visit but said nothing aqbout that. "Well, I just finished the firebird in stall three". "Firebird? I didn't see any cars. Are you doing those now"? Jim laughed. "Oh no. Not working on anybody's car. No, a client wanted his 1976 Harley mde over to resemble a 1976 Firebird. It was challenging and it's taken over a year, but it's finished, and the client is more than satisfied with it. He will pick it up Saturday morning". They walked out to stall three so Ted could get a bttr look at the bike and was quite impressed. "Man, is there anything you can't do with a bike? I've seen you turn out some great stuff, but I believe this is the best I've seen yet". Thanks Ted. I'm right proud ofit myself". They stood talking for a few minutes, then Ted go to the real reason for his visit. "I know you said your client will pick this bike up Saturay, but you got any plans for Saturday afternoon?

If you don't, I thought I'd see if you want to ride for a while. It's been a spell since I've been out, and I think I need that freedom. So, what do you say, my friend"? "Well, as far as I kow I'm free, so that sounds good to me". So with their plans made, Ted went back to the cafee to get ready for the dinner crowd. Jim went back to work, knowing that Ted hadn't gotten to the underlying reason for the invitation to ride. Not that they hadn't hit te road together before, but there had never been what he guessed what one would call and "ulterior motive" to it. But he reckoned that woulkd be revealed on their ride. Jim would just bide his time until then. In all his years on earth, biding his time was one thing he felt he'd gotten really good at doing.

Gwennie had finally settled down to work on her book but found herelf just staring at her computer screen. That morning the storyline had been so strong, but now there seemed to be nothing. She sat there for fie more minutes then decided to go for a walk. She put on her hiking boots, grabbed her walking stick and just as she stepped out her vbqack door, she heard thunder in the distance and saw that the sky was turning dark. "Well alrighty then. No writing and niow it looks like no walking either. Okay, so what to do"? She put her walking stick baqck in its place and aqnd haned back into her house shoes. It weas after five p.m. so she thought she would go ahea and start her dinner. That way if the storm did come up and knock the power out asit did sometimes, that much would be done. She washed her hands and started her grilled pork chops, brussel sprouts and baked potato. She'd had dessert at Cracker Barrel, so she wouldn't have any for with dinner. The little television was on as she worked, but she wasn't really paying attention until a "special interest" came up. It hd been about forty-eight hours since Jim had stopped the hydro-planed car, but there the driver was telling the story, and making it clear that he didn't know if he and his friends had been rescued by an angel or a sasquatch. The reporter covering the story ended the interview by asking the question; Did this really happen? And if so, who, or what, saved four people that say they were headed for certain death".

Laughing, Gwennie picked up the phone and dialed the bike shop number. "What's up my Gwennie"? She was still laughing when she asked, "So, who are you really? Are you an angel or are you Sasquatch'"? He laughed and said, "Huh? You want to come again with that"? "Remember the night you caught the car mid air and sat it down safely"? He very vividly remembered. "Yeah, I do remember, but what in the world are you talking about"? "The driver of that car was just on the local news being interviewed about that incident. So now, the questions are; (A). Are you an angel? Or (B). Are you a Sasquatch? You know my vote on that. I have always believed that you are an angel, and I will always believe that my friend". "I know that my friend, and I will always appreciate love and appreciateyou for saying that. Really, I do. But I'm just Big Jim, trying to do some good in this mean old world". And you do that very well, my friend. Well, I'll let you get back to work or whatever. Talk to you later". "Sure will". Beween thinking about the conversation with Gwennie and the ravenous hunger he uddely felt, Jim knew he wouldn't be getting any more work done. His crew had all left at five thirty, over an hour ago. So he washed his face and hands, and began to shut everything down and decided he would grab a bite to eat at Ted and Winnie's. He loved their food anyway, but he also didn't want to wait to get home and cook. He had completely forgotten to have lunch and now his stomach was telling him about himself. "I hear you, Buddy. I am going to rectifry that problem right now, so just sop yelling at me."

When Jim walked into the café, he was greeted with a hearty welcome from both Ted and Winnie. "Hey. How y'all doing this time"? They both said they were egood. "What can we get for you this evening, Jim"? "Well Winnie, I'll tell you. Everything here is so good and I'm so hungry that I feel like I could eat up all the food you got". They all laughed and and Ted and Winnie thanked him. "But for now, I think I will take a burger with all the trimmings, and iced tea. For later I think I'll have some of your good old roast beef and gravy, mashed potatoes and green beans, and two extra rolls". "You got it. I'll wait until you're ready to leave to make your plate so the food will be fresh and hot". "I appreciate that, Winnie". There wasn't a lot of conversation between the three of them after that because the dinner crowd had begun to come in. Jim mde light work of his burger, fries and tea and was soon on his way home.

Gwennie was finally doing what she had been wanting to do all day. The words were flowing now and "Please don't Pass the Sugar" was coming along quite nicely. As a matter of fact, when Jim called for their nightly conversation, he could tell that hr mind was in her character's world. He didn't mind though, as he was the same way when he had a bike he was building. There was no denying it when passion for a thing was driving you. And he was proud of his dear Gwennie. As a matter of fact, he had a copy of every book she had written and had read most of them at least twice. "Well my dear, I think your characters are calling you back into their world, so let's have a short pryer and say good night", which they did. After the qall had ended, Gwennie couldn't help but thank God once again for her precious friend, the angel named Jim. She turned bsck to her work and it was after three a.m. when she finally decided to turn in and get some sleep. She was soon nestled under her bed covers but was now wide awake. Her mind was no longer on her book, but on the lunch she would hve with Jim. She wasn't sure she wanted to have such a heavy conversation in public, remembering how it had been at the café. She decided that she would invite him to her house for lunch, that wy they would have all the freedom they needed to say whatever needed to be said and she could ask whatever needed to be asked. Unless thjere was some special reason for not doing so, she knew Jim would be good with that plan. Now, what to prepare. Jim was a huge man with a hearty appetite. She decided on stuffed pork chops, baked potatoes, spinach and rols. If he wanted dessert, she had both French vanilla and chocolate ice cream and vanilla pound cake. With her decisions mde, she set her alrm to make sure she was up early and drifted off into dreamland.

Jim was sitting in his recliner with his ever present upof coffe in his hand. Having no clue about the plans Gwennie had just made regarding their lunch the next day, he was trying to think of a quiet place they could go to where they could have thjeir much needed conversation without any chance of being overheard. Suddenly he heard, very softly, "That's already taken care of". He didn't know exactly what that meant, but he knew very well the voice that had spoken, and He trusted it, "Okay Lord. Thank You". And before long, Jim had finishe his coffee and rifted off to sleep.

The next morning was a rainy Friday. Gwennie hoped it would clear up by the time Jim came for lunch, but she knew he had ridden his bike in the rain more times than she could count. ZHe had a huge skyscraper of a truck, but he seldom drove (what other kind of truck could hold him?) It wqasn't that he didn't like his truck, he did. But he just loved his bike more. It was a 19599 Harley XLH Sportster that he had customized to comfortably accommodate his height and weight.

He'd once told her that it had taken him seven years to find that bike and another five years to customize it, but to him it was worth all the searching, all the expense and all the work he had put into it.

During their brief morning chat, she told him of her plan for lunch. "I'm making something ou love. Stuffed pork chops". "Oh man! I'm redy for that alredy. What else are you mking? Do you want me to bring nything"? "Just yourself Bif Guy along with that hearty appetite, because I'm making plenty of food counting on you to put it away, or t least carry some home for your dinner". He laughed. "You remember telling me I sometimes ct like a husband"? "Yes. Why"? "Well, you're acting like a wife". They both laughed and wished each other a great day.

Gwennie hadn't planned to write and it was a good thing too. The morning had been busy with preparing all the food, but she didn't mind one bit. Big Jim was a truly great friend to have, and he never aske for much. Now and agasin he would ask her to ride his bike with him, which she did when she could. It wasn't her fvorite ting, but he was worth the effort. At twelve -thirty sharp, she heard his skyscraper pull up in her driveway and went to open the door for Jim. "Come on in the dry. But then, with those long legs of yours, you didn't have much chance to get wet, did you"? "Nh.

And even better, you didn't have to go out and play duck with your short self today. The way it's raining I would have had to carry you like a ittle baby to keep you dry, cause with those short legs it would take you thirty minutes to walk ten feet".

They both laughed hard as they envisioned him carrying her across some parking lot into a restaurant. "Bet that would get a lot of attention", he said. "Why is that moving mountain arrying a baby doll across the parking lot"? Gwennie was now begging him to stop, as she was now crying laughing. She derly loved her friend Jim nd the relationship they shared, especially when they were laughing together. They laughed long and hard before it begasn to wind down. Gwennie, wiping her eyes, said, "Well, we have had our before lunch entertainment, so I guess it's time to eat". "Amen to that! Bring on the stuffed pork chops", Jim said rubbing his belly and licking his lips.

They didn't get into their serious conversation until they were almost done with lunch. Jim said he had cleared his afternoon so they wouldn't have to rush through their talk. "Good. Well, if you want, you can hae dinner here as well or you can take it home with you. I will never eat all this food and I only eat leftovers once. And even then, it depends on what food it is. And you know what? It feels good to have someone to cook for, other than myself". "Well my friend, with cooking for the appetite I have, you should be ecstatically happy right now". They both laughed. "I am my friend. I am very happy". Then they knew it ws time to get serious, so they moved into the den to have their talk.

"Gwennie, you already know that the dreams you've been having hd some meaning to them. And with that I'm going to sk you what might be strange question". He was quiet for so long that Gwennie asked what the question was that he wanted to ask. He was sitting facing her, so he leaned forward and asked, "Do you believe your dreams have revealed to you in any way anything about me specifically"? "I don't think so. But why are you asking me that? Are these dreams supposed to be telling me anything about you"? "I don'tsuppose so. But before we can begin the lessons, there are some things you need to know, and I know I can trust you to never reveal what I'm going to share with you. And even though I know you realy love me as a friend, you are going to find what I have to tell you unbelievable. But I solemnly promise that it's all true". For the first time in fifteen years of their friendship, Gwennie felt a little fear rising upin her. Not a fear of him, she knew he would never do anything to hurt her. She was beginning to fear what he ahd to say to her. "Gwennie, get yourself as comfortable as you can, because it's going to take a long time to tell you about me and about what's coming. So please, get whatever you nee to have by you, okay"? "Yes, I will. And I'll make you a pot of strong coffee as well". She went to the bathroom and for some reason wet a washcloth wih cold water and put it in a plastic bag to carry back into the den with her. She then put on the coffee and decided she jkust might need coffe herself, but she would start with lemonade. She knew Jim didn't care for it, he would only want his coffee.

Once she had brought in their drinks and gotten settled on her love seat, with Jim in the recliner across from her, she said, "Okay Big Fella. If you are ready to talk, I think I'm ready to listen".

"Okay. Here goes. Have you ever heard of the Nephilims I the bible"? "Yes, I have". "What do you remember about them"? They were the offspring of angels that had been with human women". Okay, good. Now, what do you know about Golisth"? "Okay, Jim. I have to ask you why we are having a bible study instead of hving our talk"? He looked at her and solemnly and said, "Gwennie, this is the beginning of our talk". Her jaw dropped and she sat speechless. He continued. "so now, lease tell me what you know or have heard of Goliath". "Well, he was a Philistine, a really big Philistine. Theologists sy he was about nine feet tall. And he is the one that David killed". "Okay". They both sat quiet for a few minutes before he finally said, "IWell, Goliath had a brother, Lemuel, who had three sons. I am many times the great grandson of Lemuel. I am the last of our kind". "Gwennie jumped up in shock. Her mind was all a-boggle. She had to walk around her house for a few minutes before she could sit back down. "Jim, yu do know that I feel ike this is a dream, right? I mean, this is incredible". She sat down and shook her head. "Okay Jim. So, I have to ask this. Just how old are you? I mean you are a descendant of Goliath, or rather his brother, then what is your tru age"? "Are you sure you cn handle it"? "Yes, I think so". "I am three hundred and forty-seven years old". Gwennie felt herself about to faint and grabbed the cold washcloth and put it to her head.

When she was more of herself, Gwennie said, "Jim, I want very much to think that you are getting back at me for calling you "older than dirt" sometimes. But I think I know you pretty well, so I know that tis is no joke. No joke at all. But three hundred forty-seven years old? How have you survived for so long? Are you the angel that I have always believed you to be? I mean, from the time you stopped that robbery in the café the day we met, I have known that you are different, but in good ways. And you know what? As strange, as bqazaar as all this is, I still feel like I know you for who you really are. I mean, it's like your age was the only thing I didn't know. Inspite of this, I can't sotp thinking of you as an angel. Jim, look at all the good you do fsor so many people. The drives you organize for the elderly and the disabled. The Thanksgiving and Christmas programs you put together and fund from your wn pocket". Now it wqas Jim's turn to be surprised. "Oh please, Jim. Did ou really think no one knew about that? I do, and I'm willing to bet there are others who at least suspect that you and you alone are the generous benefactor. Jim, you are a mountain of a man, and your heart is almost as big". That made him blush profusely, and the sight of her big friend blushing that way touched her heart deeply. He cleared his throat, then said, "You said you think you know me pretty well. I need to correct that. You know me very well, Gwennie. You are the only person that does". Now it was her turn to blush because he had made that statement with more eotion than she had ever heard or flt in any conversation they had ever had. It was as though he was trying tosay something without actually saying the words. When she trusted herself to speak, she said, "Thank you, Jim. I take that as a very high compliment". He nodded and they sat quiet for a while.

After the lunch crowd had cleared out and they could take a few minutes to sit for a little while, Ted and Winnie could finally have a conversation. "Old Man, you're looking a little tired over there. Are you okay"? "Aw yeah. I didn't sleep mucjh last night and I guess it's catching up with me". "Yes, I couldn't sleep either. That's wy I went into the guest room, so I wouldn't wake you up. Of course, at that time you were so still that I thought you were asleep". "I don't know, Win. For some reason I just can't get Jim and Gwennie off my mind. I know that whatever happened between thoe two on Wednesday is none of our business, but I can't help but feel that something was, and maybe still is very wrong. I'll tell you, I have been praying for them more than I ever have". "Me too, Honey. I'm feeling the very same way. I had meant to call Gwennie and see if we could get together today, but somehow the time just never felt right to do that". "you'll know when the time is right. In the meantime, Jim and I will be riding tomorrow afternoon. If he decides he needs and or wants to talk, I'll be there ready to do what I can". Just then, Mark, one of Jim's employees, came into the café to order lunch for the group. After he'd given Winnie the order, Ted asked, "Big Jim too busy to eat today"? They both laughed. "Naw. He had to go to Ms. Gwennie's house a while go and told us he may not be back this evening and we should close up shop". He saw the way Winnie and T4ed looked at one another and said, "Oh, it ain't no big deal. He's had to leave us to close up shop several times over the years". "Yes, I know. He always says you guys are the best employees anyone could hope to have". Mark smiled and they chatted aq little more while he waited for the food. Once Winnie handed him the ag, he said he'd see them later and was gone. They couldn't talkabout that or anything else at that time for the luch crowd had them busy, but boyj wondered why Jim had to go to Gwennie house. Once again, they both knew that none of this was their business, but they both felt even more strongly that something was wrong. They each prayed a quick and silent prayer for their dear friends.

"Okay Jim. I know you are not one toile or exaggerate or anything like that, so I know as fantastic as all this sounds, I know it's true. But I think right now, my min question is, are you human? I mean if you are three hundred and forty-seven years old, it doesn't sound like you are". He sighed and saqt still and quiet as he pondered the bet wqay to answer that question. "Honestly, I know very little about my family history. Of the stories I have been told, and this was a very long time ago, over three hundred years. So I have had to piece together the story, just to try to figure out who I really am. I never knew my parents. My father apparently disappeare shortly after I was born. Family members said he was aq great hunter and they think he may have strayed too for from their village and was slain. After the whole David and Goliath thing, we were all labelled as enemies of God, so it was okay to kill our people off whenever anyone got the chance to do it. I was told that three days after my father disappeared, my mother died. Anyway, I remember that I was the "Village Kid", everyone took part of my upbringing. That was good, but even though I belonged to the village, there were times when I felt that I didn't belong to anyone. Anyway, back then we lived mostly in caves in one city or another in Palestine, also known as Canaan. It was told that one of our earliest forefathers swore that he was a descendant of the Nephilim, but others in the family say we are Anakim, a race of giants descended from Anak. Apparently, none of my family really knew anything about Anak, except that he seems to have been the, or at least one of the forefathers of the giants. There weren't a lot of children born among our people so between being killed and low birth rate, my people died out. Or, if there are others, I have never known about them. When I was about one hundred

Big Jim

and sixty-two years old, I decided I was tireof cave dwelling and living only among my own dying race, so I left one day, just walking. I learned pretty quickly what a lot of the world was like for people like me. So, I learned to stick to the shadows as much s I could, but still stay closely enough to learn about other people and how they lived. At first, iirst it was scary. When men would see me, they wanted to kill me, most of them anyway. Women and children always screamed and ran. I not only felt alone. I really was alone and wondered if I had made a mistake in not continuing to live in our caves. It's just that I knew there had to be more. I wondered how long we would have to suffer for what my uncle Goliath had done and the reputation he had brough upon us. I knew there had to be more. Anyway, I kept walking hunting and eating what I could find. It was a lonely life so as you can imagine I dida lot of thinking along the way. I began to think about stories my people had told around the campfire at night, paying special ayyrnyion to the stories about Uncle Goliath. It was said that he was the strongest of them all and was the best warrior, that no one messed with our people while he was alive". Jim stopped talking for a minute, then said, "My Gwennie, I think I need a cup of good, strong coffee to finish telling you this". I'll get it for you", Gwennie said, thinking she needed a brak from hearing his story. That was quite a lot to wrap your head around. A little more and she could believe she was listening to someone read a book. But pour Jim wasn't reading a book; this was his life story. And it was a sad one. Her heart wet out for her friend even more. She shook her head and carried his coffee in to him. "Here you go my friend". "Thank you Gwennie. I appreciate it". After taking a few sips of the hot coffee, Jim continues to ell his story. "Now back to my life journey thus far. As I wondered, never really knowing where I was, I thought more and more about the terrible stigma that had been on my family for so long. Then I began to wonder if there was any way I could change that. More and more I believed there just had to be a way, and that I was the only one that could find it. So, I walked. I thought. I learned along the way. Believe it or not, I had been walking for over a hundred years when I first heard about God, the heavenly God, t least, since I had heard about Hm and David. I didn't know where I was, and I didn't fully understand the language. But as I traveled, I did learn some basics of some language. It was later that I learned that I was in England. And you know what? Those people accepted me for the most part. My size didn't seem to bother them. In fact, a man named Doald Beardsley, a tall man himself, took me taught me how to dress like everyone else and gave me a job as a carpenter. That's when I discovered that I love working with my hands. He believed strongly in God, so I began to ask questions about Him. I never told him my family's history though for fear I would lose the only friend I had made since leaving home. Well anyway, the more I learned about

God and about Jesus, the more I felt I had found he way to do something that would finally bring some good to the family name of Goliath. Mr. Beardsley had taught me that when he prayed, he was having a conversation with Who he called "my Lord", and he told me I could do the same. So, I began to talk to Him. In the ginning I didn't know what to say or how to say it. I wqsn't sure He was even listening. But I kept begging Him to show me what I could do to lift the stigma off my people, even though as fr as I knew they were all gone. I had been in England learning all I could from Mr. Beardsley for about twelve years when Mr. Beardsley died. He was only eighty-three yers old. And during those twelve years I had known others in their village to die young, some even younger than mr. Beardsley. As far I knew, the only way anyone in my family died under one hundred was when they were killed. So, I began to wonder how it was that we normally lived so long. I still can't answer that question. I know we are not angels of any sort. Well, when my only real friend had died, I was alone again, and it hurt deeply, more than anything I had ever experienced. That's when I began to pray in earnest. I had learned so much in my travels, but mr. Beardsley was the onl one that really talked o me about God, about Jesus, and gave me hope to do some good in this world. I asked God to please let me work for Him, and it wsn't long before I found myself in positions to help others. All of a sudden, I could move wth a swiftness I had never known before. We have always been a strong people, but I found that I had even more strength. I stil walked across the land, learning more about God, about people, their lands, and about myself. Sixty years ago I was about two hundred eighty-seven years old when I found myself here. For some reason I felt like I was finaly home, so I settled here. I had worked odd jobs to earn money along the way, mostly as a carpenter. But it's here that I l earned about birth certificates, social security numbers, taxes and motorcycles. I had no idea what to do or how to do it. But God sent the people I needed to help me with all of it. None of them asked too many questions. I could tell they knewI was being vague on my age, where I was from, things like that. But all through the process, I knew that God was with me. Once I had my documents, I got a job repairing cars and motorcycles, and I found myself learning quickly and loving it, especially working with the motorcycles. Ten years later I was able to buy both my house and the shop from the previous owner. He had decided to retire so he and his wife could move to Florida. I met Ted and Winnie when they first opened the café, and we became friends. I got involved with the community because I love it here and most of the people here are friendly and caring, hardworking folks. Nd, I believe it to be one of the ways God has given me to do some good. You know, I don't know if it's possible to change what people think and say about my people, but what I do know is that God has been very good to me. I don't know why He chose to bless me with such speed, or the ability to know hen I am supposed to be somewhere to help someone in need, or with exceptional strength, except say He heard my pryer and is letting me do what I can to show Him that I am sorry for what happened all those years ago s well as for any wrong I do along the way. And one way I know He heard my prayer is that I wanted another very special friend. It had been so long that I had felt alone, even though I had acquaintances and a few friends, I just needed that one person I could talk to about anything. That one friend that would love and accept me for who I am, not for my size. And I thank God for answering that prayer by sending you into my life". Gwennie's heart was full and so were here eyes. Jim tried to wipe way the tears away but they were flowing too fast for him to keep up with them. In true Gwennie form, she said, "Thank you my friend, but I think this is a job for Kleenex". They both chuckled, though a little sadly. Then they sat quietly for almost thirty minutes before either of them said a word. Finally, Gwennie said, "I can't begin to imagine how all those years must have been for you. I mean, leaving your home and having to learn firsthand about new cultures, about the people and their lands. And not only that, but to have crossed over time as well. And alone almost that whole time. Wow". She stopped talking and shook her head, then said, "Wait a minute. Your driver's license can't show your true age, so how old do you say you are on here? On there I am now sixty-four". "Hmm. Okay, you actually can pass for that. I know one thing. I won't be teasing you about being older than dirt anymore". "Gwennie, please don't change. I love the way we are in our relationship and if you wer to chanfe in any way, I think we would lose something very precious". "Okay my friend. I hear you. But I do have a question. Are you sure about your age? I mean with all the wqalking and traveling across years and centuries, how have you been able to keep up with it"? "That's a very good question. In the beginning, when the sun came up, I would find a stick and write in the sand to remind myself of my age. I'm sure I may have missed some days here and there, but according to what little information I ever got from my family, I know I am in the neighborhood of three hundred and forty-seven". "That's amazing. You don't look or move like it, especially when you move like lightening". She shoojk her hea and said "Boy would a lot of women love to know that secret. I mean, you could pass for your sixties, and when you clean up, you could even appear to be in your fifties. You really do look good for your age Jim". "Thank you". He looked at the clock on the mantle and saw that his crew would soon be closing shop. "Wow. I didn't realize it was this late", he said. She looked at the same clock and asked, "Do you have to leave now"? "Well, the fellas will lock up. They have done it several times before". "Good. Then you can sta for supper and yu know me well enough to know that I won't take no for an answer". He laughed and said,

"Yes. I do know just how bossy you are", and they both laughed and went into the kitchen for supper.

As they ate, Gwennie asked, "So, what are we doing after supper? Do you finish blowing my mind with what's going on with my dreams and what you know is coming"? Jim thought for a moment, then said, "I've been thinking about that. I know I have poured so much information on you today, I think maybe we need to wait a day or two before we can go any further. I think maybe you need to get your head wrapped around all I have told you. So, how about waiting until Tuesday or Wednesday to start"? Gwennie thought for a minute, then said, "Well, I thnk that's for you to say. Afer all, you know what has to be done. All I know for sure is that we can't wait too long t get this done. So, are there any special exercises or something that I need to start doing to begin preparing for this"? "Well, you already do a lot of walking. Other than that, are there any other exercises that you do"? Wednesday afternoon"I do some stretches. Sometimes I dance. You know, just to get th heart pumping. But that's mostly when I'm cleaning or cooking. And sometimes when I'm walking, I may do a little dancing along the path". He laughed. "I can see you doing that, too". After the laughter, they decided that the lessons would begin on Wednesday afternoon, which was fine with Gwennie. It was what he said next that shocked her. "I have to begin teaching you how to silence your mind as well as your mouth". She gasped, and he thought she had been offended by his remark. "Oh, no. I'm not calling you a "big muuth" or anything like that. It's just...". She interrupted him and said, "It's not that. It's just that when I was walking the other day, I can't remember which, I hear that very same thing. I heard that I have to learn to silence my mind and my mouth. I remember being told to focus on the quiet in the woods. And now, to hear you say that, well, it just surprised me, that's all". Now it was Jim's turn to be shocked. It seemed to Him that god had already begun the lessons that Gwennie needed to learn.

After supper was over and Jim had helped Gwenni clean the kitchen, they webt back inyo the den and decided they wanted to find a good comedy to watch. Not finding a movie they were interested in, they settled on Sanford and Son. Fred Sanford was always good for a laugh, especially when he an Esther were having one of their arguments. After almost two episodes of the show, Gwennie asked, "Ji, I have just got to ask this. Wha ddid you think the first time you saw a television"? He laughed long nd hard, which let Gwennie know that there was definitely an interesting story in that answer. When he could control his laughter enough to abswer he said, "I was over in Dunsford attending a vintage car and bike show. After seeing all the vehicles and talking to ome of the owners, I thought I would walk through the small town before heading home. Out of the corner ofmy eye, I saw movement. When I turned, I saw a man holding a gun and it seemed to be aimed at me. So, thinking to avoid any rfeal trouble, I put my hand out to take the gun away. I broke the plate glass window and the screen of the television. I know I must have looked like the world's biggest fools. All I could do was stand their gaping at the damage I'd done and wonder what had happened to the litte man that had aimed his gun at me. When the police and the shop owner arrived and saw my size, they stood there gping at me just as much as I gaped as I had been gaping at the destruction. Finally, the sheriff asked"Big fella, What in the world did you do that for"? I explained that I had seen a little man aiming his gun at me and that all I had meant to do was take it away from him, but that he had just disappeared after all the glass broke. They laughed, but I didn't see anything funny. I really did want to know how that ittle man got away. Finally, the shop owner said, "What you beojke big fella, other than my store window that is, is called a tekevision. The little man you saw wasn't real. At least not like we are. He was in a moving picture inside the television and the show was probably a western"? "A western? Moving pictures? You mean pictures like you would take with camera"? The men looked at each other and the sheriff said, "Well, yes and no. It's a little hard to explain. Look fella, what's your name and where are you from"? "I'm James Beardsley and I'm from Rock Run, two towns over". "Okay. Well now, it's up to old Doc Martin here as to whether he wants to pres charges against you". Doc had arrived filled with aner, but after they had heard Jim's explanation as to what had happened, Doc felt sorry for him. He had the feeling that there was more to the big man's story than he was telling. He had never in his life seen a man that big, nor ha he ever seen one that seemed so, well, out of touch with life as it was. It was as if thi man was some giant from another time and place. "Well, I'll tell you what James Beardsley. If you promise to pay for my window and the television, I won't press chatges". He laughed said, "IEven if I wanted to, I just don't see you fitting in the jail anyway. You're the biggest man I have ever seen. Leave your name, address and phone number and after I get the estimates for the window, I'll let you know what you owe me, how's that"? "That sounds fine to me, Sir. I will glad pay for the damage I did, and I want to apologize to you right now". They talked for a while afer Jim told them that he hd originally came to their town for the casr and bike show and decided to walk around the town since he's never been there before. Two weeks later Jim had been called with the amount of money he owed. He closed his shop and went straight to the bank, then to Doc's shop to py his bill. They didn't quite become frien, but Jim would stop in and say hello whenever he was in Dunsford, and Doc had always welcomed him and asked him to have qa cup of coffee. He had even taqught Jim hjow to play checkers.

 Gwennie had laughed hard as Jim regaling her with that story. What mde it s funny was that not only coud she picture him as he told it, but he was using hand motions to telli it. He had often told her funny things over the years, but nothing as funny as this. She had laughed so hard that she was crying just as he had been before he could start to answer her question. Not only was she crying, but her head, sides and abdomen hurt from lauhbg so much and so hard. But it felt good though. She had the fleeting thought that once they started the lessons, they may not get many opportunities to laugh like that again, and once this battle or war, or whatever it was began she was almost positive there would be no laughter.

Jim, laughing himself, thought "I really love to hear my Gwennie laugh. It's such a free and happy sound. An infectious sound. You didn't even have to know what she is laughing at, and you'll find yourself laughing with her". Aloud, he said, "You know what? Your laughter is one of my greatest joys in life. In all my years on earth, I have never heard anyone else laugh in such a way as yo do. I really wish I had a way to fill you with so much joy that you would never stop laughing. I mean that". Soberly, Gwennie looked at him and said, "I know you mean it my friends. And I thank you for being my true, loyal and loving friend". Then she did something she had never done in all fifteen years of their friendship. She walked over to where he was sitting, hugged him and kissed his righ cheek. "I love you my dear friend. I never want to lose you or the relationship we so much enjoy". She kissed his cheek again, then went back to her place on the loveseat. They both sat quiet for a few minutes, each thinking their own thoughts. A stunned Jim sar rhnking, "Wow. I never expected my Gwennie to do that, but it sure was nice. I kind os wish she would do that more often. I wonder how she would feel if I returned the favor. Better not. As much as I have wanted to do something like that for a lot of years, I'd better not. Best not to open a door I know I can't walk through. So, I'll just keep it like it is. I'll just ettle for continuing to wonder and imagine". He hoped he sounded like he was joking when he said, "Now my left cheek feels left out. You need to kiss that one and then run away quick". "Okay, but why do I need to run away quick"? "Even though it would beon your cheek as well, can yu just imagine a mountain kissing a little China doll? I'm so big, my mouth would cover your whole head". And there they were laughing again, as they both imagined what he had described. Once again Gwennie found herself thinking This may be the last really good laughter they get to have together for a long time. And once again Jim thought he ahd the power to keep her laughing forever. When the laughter died down, they finalized their plans to begin her lessons on Wednesday afternoon. Jim looked at his watch and saw that it was almost eleven p.m., the latest he's ever stayed at her house. "Oh mn! It's late. I'd better get out of here. I hope I haven't overstayed my welcome". "Never my friend. Never". "Thanks Gwennie. And thank you for al that good food. That was some mighty fine cooking". "And I thank you for saying so. We'll have to do it again soon". "Yeah, but only after I've taken you out to about ten meals. It feels like I ate up a lest that much food". "Hey, that's why I cooked so much. I wanted yu to come with a hearty appetite and I'm so glad you didn't disappoint me". "Well, thanks again. I'd beter say good and head on home. I have to meet a customer in ehe morning and Ted and I are supposed to ride tomorrow afternoon". 'Well, be safe and enjoy. Good night my friend". On his wayhome, Jim couldn't stop thinking about Gwennie kissing him on the cheek and just how sweet and special it had made him feel. It was then that he remembered that she hdn't kissed his left cheek, they had been laughing too hard at the thought of a mountain kissing a China doll. "Oh well, maybe that was for the best". As he stepped into his house, he thought, "If only....", and forced himself to let that trail of thinking fall by the wayside. Again, he thought, "No need opening I can't walk through. Still, sometimes I wonder how she would react if she knew the truth but his feelings for her. Oh no. There I go thinking of opening doors again".

As she was getting comfortable for the night and was preparing to write for a while, Gwennie thought about Jim and their whole evening together. He had never stayed at her house that long. The longest he had ever stayed was about two hours and even that was a very rare thing. Then she thought about her impulse to hug him and kiss his cheek. In the fifteen yeas they'd been friends they had hugged of course, but not often. And there had never been any kisses of any kind. She loved Jim dearly and, though she would never tell him so, she had always felt a little sorry for him. Even ub tgus twentieth century there were still people who couldn't simply accept others for who they were and not jdge them fr their size, their skin color, their clothes or any of the superficial stuff. He had told her once that over the years, he hadn't told er how many, people in general had begun to either accept him or see him as a walking oddity, which he really didn't mind. What he absolutely hated was for men or young boys to try to provoke him to fight. And it bbroke his heart when little children wanted to come close to him out of curiosity and their parents would quickly call them away as though he was a monster of some sort. Sometimes he thought that maybe he did look like a monster s big as he was. He'd stopped walking through the park for that very reason. He loved children and wanted to play ball with them or push them on the merry-go-round. Yes, her friend, Big Jim was a very speial man. And while it was true that he now fit into society, he was still misunderstood at times. Most people just left him alone, but if they had only taken the time to get to know him, and to know how big his heart was they would also seejust how much love that big heart contained, she was sure they would be friendlier, more open to hm.

As Gwennie and Jim laughed at the "mountain and the China doll" joke Ted and Winnie were closing

Big Jim

the café. All the employees had left for the night and Ted and Winie had locked up and were now heading home themselves. They had both been wondering if Gwennie was okay but hadn't had a chance to talk and wonder together. But eah of them whispered short little prayers for both Gwennie and Jim as often as they could. Now, on the ride home, Winnie siaid, "I sure hope Gwennie is okay. I mean, for Jim to leave the shop and go to her house like that. It just makes me feel that something is very wrong. I wanted to call her, but we were so busy that I never had a chance to. And well, I guess maybe that was how I should have been. I guess it really wasn't for me to come off to her as being a nosey-rosey". "Well, I guess we both wanted to be nosey. I had thought about calling Jim's house and asking if we were still rifing tomorrow, hoping that if we did get to talk maybe I would find out if anything was wrong with Gwennie. But like you said, I guess it really was just none of our business. Except, like you, I can't shake the feeling that something is wrong. Very wrong". "Well, I guess you 'll at least have some idea tomorrow if everything is okay'. Then changing te subject, Winnie said, "I sure am glad we ate before leaving the café. I don't think I could cook one more thing tonight. I am so grateful for our customers, but it keeps us hopping". They both chuckled. "And if puts food on our own table". He laughed at his joke; Winnie giggles a little bit. "But seriously. Before we go to sleep, I'd like us to join hands and pray for our friends Him and Gwenie". Certainly Dear. I'd like that too" Winnie replied. They went on to to talk about various things that needed to be done the next day at the café. But all the while Ted was wondering why he and Winnie were so "overly" concerned about Jim and Gwennie. Were they just being nosey, or was there something behind the curiosity he and Winie shared? Without realizing itit he said out loud, "Well, one thing's for sure. God and time will tell". Winnie asked incredulously, "About the new veggie order"? "Hm? Oh, no. I guess I was thinking out loud". Winnie didn't have to ask what, or rather who, her dear husband was thinking of.

Jim had been home for ovr an hour. He had known that he wouldn't be able to sleep, so he made a pot of coffee and sat in his recliner to read a while. He picked up Gwennie's lastest book, "Am I Even in My Life?" He chuckled as he began to read. Gwennie's books always had strange, attention getting titles and they were written with humor, yet they were filled with nuggets of wisdom. Four pages into the book, he began remembering their evening together. He'd never spent that much time at her house, and especially had never stayed that late. But they had needed tha time together. She neede to know as much about him as possible. For such an ensuing battle as they were facing, trust was a major must. And it would help when he needed her to be able to read him, calculate his next moves without him having to say a word verbally. She had already been told that she must learn to silence her mind and her mouth. Most people fooound it much easier to control their mouth han it was to control the mind. The mind can be like a speeding freight train; full speed ahead with n brakes to stop it, not even an emergency brake. He would give her pointers n that, but that was one of thoe things no one could do for another person. Each individual had to find their own way to silence their mind. Him laid the book to the side. Just for now, he needed to silence his own mind. He had talked more about himself to Gwennie than he hd ever done. Added to that, he wondered what had made her suddenly hug him, nothing really new in that. But she hd never kissed him before, even on the cheek. He hoped with all his heart that he hadn't given away his true feelings for her. She didn't behave any differently afterwards, so he thought maybe he had played that just right by joking with her. He thought about the coming battle they would have to fight. Aloud he said, "Lord, as old as I am, there is still so much that I still don't know. I know the things I learned back in Canaan, things the men in my family taught me about hunting and fighting. And I know things You have been gracious enough to teach me. And I know there is no one else to help her with this. But Lord, are You sure that I know enough to teach her all she needs to know? I mean she is getting ready for this battle and at the same time she must learn her own true identity. That's a whole lot to put on her at one time." He got up and begn to walk through his house, thankful that he lived alone.

As bid and heavy as he way, he was not a person that could tip around to keep from waking anyone up. "I jsust don't want to mess this up, Lord. There is just too much at stake. And Gwennie. My Gwennie". He didn't realize that tears had begun to run down his cheeks. "Lord, I have to get this right for her sake especially. I can't let anything happen to her. I mean, I am grateful that you saw fit to give me life and that You love me despite the reputation my family gined because f Uncle Goliath. It's been a hard, lonely life, but it got better after I got to know about You and then to know You. But since you've brought my Gwennie into my life things have been so much sweeter. It seems like the sun staared shining more brightly. She has given this old mountain of a man reasons to love, as best I can anyway. She brings joy and laughter ino my life. Oh, I already knew that marriage was out of the question for so many reasons. I am just too old and too big for all that. I can trust her so I can tlk to her about anything, well, except how I truly feel about her. Lord, I know yhat when we are born and when we die is for You to say, but I can't let anything happen to Gwennie. I can't let her die, especially if I did something wrong to cause her death. If either of us has to die in this battle, let it be me. I have lived an awfully long time, she hasn't. And I wouldn't want to live anymore if she wereto die. So now, do you see why I m asking You t help me do this thing right? I'm trusting You to help me Lord". He thought about going to bed but knew he still wouldn't be able to sleep. So, he got himself a fresh pot of coffee and settled in his recliner to see if there was anything worth waqtching on television.

It was three seventeen on Saturday morning and Gwennie was wide awake. She had at some point drifted off to sleep, but she had a weird dream. She was first dreaming that she was running on the trail behind her house, when all of a sudden, she heard other footsteps on the path. She turned to see who was there but saw no one. She turned back around but decided to walk instead of running. She walked slowly and deliberately so that ever who was there wouldn't think she ws afraid. Dhe hadn't had her walking stick when she ws running, but it hd now appeared in her hand. She was carrying it in a way that she could quickly swing on anyone that tried to approach her. When she headed back to the house, she heard the footsteps again and agin they were behind her. She turned to look, but again, no one was there She picked up the pae and did a brisk walk back to her house. Just as she approached the edge of her back yard, she felt something or someone lunge at her, and that was when she woke up. She laid there breathing hard and sweating as though she had actually been running, as she wondered if that dream had any correlation to the dreams, she had about her and Jim walking and carrying those swords.

CHAPTER EIGHT

Jim hadn't slept at all. He just thought and prayed all night. He stood up, stretched and headed for the shower. As he turned on rhe water, he chuckled as he remembered how it was when he ha first bought the house. It hsd twelve-foot ceilings, so that was okay. It had been the bathroom and doorways that absolutely had to be changed, so he got to work, thanking God for Mr. Beaqrdsley, who had taught him arpentry so long ago. Between working at the shop and remodeling his house, it had been over a year before he could walk in without having to crouch down, and comfortable fit in his bathroom. He thought about his family. If any of them hd a wqay to see him all these centuries and years later, they probably would turn over in their graves, as the old saying goes. In the caves there were no kitchens and bathrooms, no running water. And he couldonly imagine what it would be like if they knew about electricity and electrical appliances. And don't mention television. Jimwas bad enough, but they probably would have yelled out "divination", saying it ws the devil's doings. But then, in all honesty, he wouldn't be able to talk, because he wasn't very much better. He had encountered and experienced many new things over the years. And that included new people. Until he had left his home, he had only encountered people like him. So whenhe saw other people and how small they were compared to him, he at first had thought he was seeing things. Were they devils pr angels? He didn't know at that time. But over the years, the more he travelled and had encountered so many different reactions when people saw him, he figured they couldn't be either, because he thought neither abges nor demons would fear him. So, they had to be people, just different from him and his people. He had been in his late one hundreds all those years ago. All those years ago. And as he dressed, he wondered once again for maybe the millionth tie just why he ha lived so long. He knew how, it was God keeping him on earth. But he just didn't know why. He had learned from the bible that there had been people back then that lived even longer. One mn named Methuselah had lived to be nine hundred and sixty-nine years old. He said alour, "Oh well Lord. That's Your business. My business is simply to do Your will". Once he was dressed, he got a cup of coffee, then went to the phone to give Gwennie his usual "good morning" call. "Good morning, Big Jim. How are you this fine morning"? I'm good, my Gwennie. How are you? How'd you sleep"? "I'm good, thanks. How about you"? She had said she was good, but he could tell that she wasn't. "realy am good, but I'm getting the feeling that you aren't. Not really. Anything you need or want to talk about"? "I don't really know. I had a strange dream and I am trying to figure out if it has a meaning. I feel like it does". Jim felt a knot form in the pit of his stomach. "Was it anything like the others"? "No. Thisone was totally different. But I know you have to get to your shop now, so I'll tell you later, okay"? "Okay my Gwennie. Well, letr's play a quick prayer", which they did. After saying "Amen", Jim said, I'll checxk on you later in case you need me", "Okay my friend. Thanks, and enjoy your day". "Thanks, you too". Jim ooked at his watch and saw that it was fst approchng eight, so he needed to hightail it to the shop. He had a special client to meet and a rather lucrative paycheck to collect. But even more importantly to Him, he loved seeing the faces of any of his well satisfied customers. That meant so much more to him than the money, which was good. Everybody needed money to live, but his needs were minimal, mostly just the basic needs. He wasn't interested in men's latest clothing fashions. Because of his size all his clothes had to be custom made from simple patterns. Even his biking gear was custom made. His shoes were seventeen D, hard to find but find them he always did, mostly biker boots. So, yes, his needs weren't that many, and his wants were simple enough. God had blessed him with all he needed and more. So, even though the money he got paid from building custom bikes was always a quite healthy sum, the joy he saw in his customets' faces meant so much more to him. His other joy was knowing that when he left this world, his Gwennie would then own everything he had. When he hd first told her what he wanted to do, she had protested, only giving in when he reminded her that he had no one else to leave everything too.

Ted had seen the joy on the face of Jim's customer. That was a man that absolutely loved what he was looking at and anticipated riding. And Jim, though he wasn't a money hungry sort, had to be a happy camper himself. One of his employees had told Ted that particular bike was over a million dollars. Ted could believe it. When Jim had showed it to him, he saw all the detail that had gone into building that bike. Tht same employee ha told Ted that no customized bike Jim sold went for less than half a million dollars. But to look at Big Jim, you could make the mistake of assuming that he didn't have two nickels to rub together. What a mistake to make. Once the bike was loaded and the customer had driven away, Ted asked Jim if they were still riding later. "Oh yeah Man. I'm definitely ready for a good ride today. Syill at two"? "Yep, but I heard you had to go over to Gwennie's yesterday, so I wasn't sure if something was wrong with her, and well, she might need you to stick around". Jim deliberately chose to not respond, and Ted didn't miss that either. Ted and Winnie were good people, and they were friends, but nowhere near being the friends that his Gwennie was to him. He figured they didn't need to know what was ging on. Well, everything at the café is set. Big Billy is working today, so if there is any troule, he will handle, so I'll be out to ride then". Ted wasn't worried about leaving Winnie in the café as long as her younger brother, Big Billie was there with her. He was six feet, four inches tall, two hundred and fifty pounds, all muscle. And that big fell absolutely adored his "Big Sis" and allowed no one to mess with her when he was around.

He had never been one to sart fights but neither had he ever been one to not finish a fight. And he adored his "Big Sis", so he would protect her at all costs. But everything should be fine. They very rarely had any trouble and the last time anyone had attempted to rob them was fifteen years ago, and it had been Big Jim that had foiled that one. That was the day that he and Gwennie had met, the day that their friendship had begun.

Jim thought e would do some paperwork and neaten up the shop while he waite to ride. When his stomach let out a thunderous growl, he remembered that he hadn't had breakfast which was very unusual. He thought about going next door to the café but decided against it. He knew Ted had meant no harm with his "fishing expedition" about Gwenie, but Jimi didn't want to go through that same thing with Winnie. He knew that even though she and Gwennie were friends, they weren't that close. And even if they had been, he still felt that what was going on with him and Gwennie ws not anyone else's business. He had lived long enough to know that even good people could unknowingly be agents of the devil. And he and Gwennie had enough to deal with, no need to risk adding to that. Having made his decision, he waited as long as he coud to eat, thinking that he and

Ted usually stopped on the road to sit and eat and talk. He's just make up for lost time then. But suddenly his stomach let out a growl that refused to be ignored. He felt that if his stomach had way to get outside of his body, he would have quite a fight on is hands. He laughed as he envisioned a fight like that. He patted his belly and said, "Okay Buddy, you win. Let's go get you some food right now". He looked at his watch and saw it wasn't quite noon, and he and Ted wouldn't even e leaving until two. So, Jim figured his stomach had a right to yell at him. "I don't want any questions about my Gwennie, ut I guess I'd better put that aside for now".

As soon as he walked into the café, Big Nilly said, "Well, hello there, "Bigger than me", which was his name for Jim. "How are ya these days"? "Hello Billy. I'm good, Man. But I think I'm about to get beat up by my stomach though". They and some other customers laughed at that. An older gentleman sitting at a nearby table said, "Well young fella, you'd better eat soon. I'd hate to see a bgg fella like you get knocked out by his own stomach". That brought such a loud and hearty round of laughter that both Ted and Winnie came out to see what was so funny. Winnie spoke to Jim and asked, "What in the world is so funny out here"? Jim said, rather matter fof factly, "Oh, we're kust talking a stomach knocking someone out". That brought more laughter that left Ted nd Winnie smiling at one another but puzzled. Finally, Jim explained what all the laughter was about, then place his order. He was glad to see that Winnie went back into the kitchen with Ted. Jim still didn't want the supposedly subtle questions about his Gwennie, and for the time he was there, he didn't get those questions. There were so many customers that Te and Winnie were both too busy to talk to anyone. Seeing just how full and busy the café was, Jim asked Ted if he still wanted to rride, but it was Winnie that answered. "Yes, Jim. He needs that, so get him out of here and you both enjoy". "Yes ma'am", Jim replied with a smile.

Back in his shop, Jim thought he would call Gwennie and see what she was up to. "Hello my friend. Has your customer been and gone"? "Oh yeah. That satisfied customer left a few hours ago". Then he went on to tell her about the joke of his stomach beating him up. She laughed, but not like he thought she normally would have. "Alright my Gwennie. Is something wrong? I can tell you aree not quite yourself. You don't have that sleepy sound, so I know I didn't wake you up or anything like that. So, again, what's wrong"? "It is so amazing that you know me so well. And I'm grateful for that. But I'm good my friend. I just have so many thoughts running around in my head. Some about our conversation, some about the new book. And for some reason, I'm thinking a lot about my parents, wishing they were still here. So, you see my friend, I'm well, just being human, I guess. I mean we all have our periods of deep thoughtfulness, don't we"? When she had said she was thinking about their conversation, he knew that she was talking about the day before. He knew he ha laid a lot of heavy stuff in her lap and wasn't surprise that it was still fresh on her mind. "Gwennie, I know I laid a lot on you yesterday. An awful lot. And I know a lot of it was really hard to wrap your head around. If I hadn't lived it, I think maybe I would think someone had an overly active imagination. So it's quite alright if you are having a hard time believing that it's all reall". "No, it's not that, Jim. As incredulous as it all sounds, I know you ae not a liar. And even though you can be given to imagination at times, it's just not wild enough for you to make up something like that. No, it's just that, well, and I know you won't like this, but I can't help feeling so sad for you. I mean, so many of us think we have it hard, and sometimes we do. But I'm just more mindful of just how blessed I am. I mean, 347 years and most of that you have been alone. No wife, no children and very few friends. And I can't even imagine what it must be like to know that you are the last of your people". She suddenly thought about all she was saying and stopped talking. Then she said, "Oh Jim I am so sorry. I'm not trying to bring you down. I want you to enjoy your day, enjoy your ride with Ted. So, forgive me, okay"? At that moment Jim's heart was filled with more love for his Gwennie than he had ever felt. And he had felt her love for him more strongly than he had in the whole fifteen years of their friendship. He had to struggle to fight back the tears, so he had to stay silent for a couple of minutes. "Jim, are you upset? He cleared his throat, then said, "No my Gwennie, I'm upset. It's just that, we;;, like you said, I have been alone for more of my life than I care to remember. But knowing I have been blessed with you, my very bv bst friend, well, it's like you have been with me a lifetime, if that makes any sense at all. And I thank you for loving me so much. I certainly don't take that for granted". "Hey, that goes both ways my friend. I'm grateful to have you in my life as well"> She thougt their conversation was too heavy for a bright sunny Saturday. Especially when he was supposed to do one thing he absolutely loved to do. "You know what, my friend? We are getting to sappy for such a beautiful Saturday. I don't want anything to spoil your "freedom on the road", she said with a laugh. He thought her life was better than before, but still not her normal, infectious laughter. " Aww, it will still be good. And while we are on the subject, you haven't been on the bike with me in quite a while. Don't you owe me a ride"? He laughed when she replied, "Man, I don't owe you no rde on oo bike, so don't even try it". Now, that was his Gwennie in rue form, and that made him feel better. They were both laughing now, and it was her true laughter he heard. Then she said, "Maybe next Saturday I'll ride with you if it's not raining". I'm holding you to that". "Hey! I said "maybe" I would". "Oh well, that "maybe" must have run right past my ears then". They laughed again, then daid they would talk later and she, as always cautioned him to stay safe. He would do just that.

After the call had ended, Gwennie thought she would take a walk. As she headed out her back door, whe remembered her dream and wondered if it was warning her that something like that would really happen. Or could it have been some new twist to the dreams she'd been having about he coming battle she nd Jim were about to prepare for? She didn't know, but she would not live in fear. She loved walking the trail behind her house, had done it for years, nd she wasn't about to sop walking now. But just in case, she carried her baseball bat as ell as her walking stick. The bat was in its little carrying bag she had made for it, so she slung it over her shoulder and started her walk. She started dancing and singing "Ain't no stopping us now", substituting the word "me" for "us". She was about halfway down the trail when she thought/hear/felt that she needed to be still and quiet. So, she turned back so she could sit on the stump she had been sitting on when she had heard that she had to learn how to silence her mind and her mouth. She guessed it was time for another lesson, so she sat down and softly sked the Lord, will

You please help me with this? I think I'm good with silencing my mouth. I've had to do that lot of times. But my mind, Lord. How in the world can I silence my mind, if You don't show me how"?

She sat quietly th her eyes closed for a few seconds as she inhaled deeply and and exhaled slowly. She tried to will her mind to be still, be silent, but was having trouble with that. She remembered that before she had been directed to focus on the silence in the woods. Of course, there were irds singing, all the normal sounds you jear outside and she was so used to those sounds that she barely noticed them any mre. But thjere were no people, no vehicles of ny kind and now she was urning the volume on her phone completely down. Now once again she was sitting quiet and motionless, willing her mind to obey her command to be silent. She focused on the quietness of he woods again and found her mind being quieted. Suddenly she found herself entering another world, or was it another realm? She wasn't sure and she also wasn't sure just what was happening t her. It was as though she was drifting away from the world she knew and into a strange new one. But if so, who or what was there waiting for her? Ever what, she felt no fear, at least none that registered within her any way. As a matter of fact, nothing she knew andwas familiar with registered to her. It was as though nothing and no oneelse existd. Suddenly she saw, what had to be angels smiling and beckoning her to come forward, which she did. They led her to what appeared to be an ancient battlefield. She didn't know how she knew that, but she did. All of a suddebn, a huge whiete hore bearing a huge rider trotted up to her. It was crazy, but the horse was so white that he seemed to sparkle and glow. And the way the animal approached her, it was like he knew her; he even seemed to nod his hea to speak to her. She said "Hello, bit fella. You are a beauty". She looked up at the rider, wondering if all the angels were that big. Then the angel spoke. Hello Gwenie. Do you have any ide where you are". "No, I don't. And may I ask your name"? "My name is not important, but I am an anel of war and I hsave always watched over you, as I will be with you and watch over you when you go into battle". He motioned for her to give him her hand and he took her up onto the horse's back, then told her to take a good look around. Gwennie, this is the Elah Valley, where David conquered Goliath. Here is where you will learn about the weapons you must use and how ot use them correctly. These weapons are nothing like the weapons of your world and time. But we know you will learn and develop quickly, for you are a very determined and persistent warrior. Always have been. I will be watching as Jim instructs you. He is from a lineage of of strong and wise hunters and warriors. He knows much and can do much. What you have seen him to is only a tiny porion of warrior abilities he has been given. Some of those abilities Gvenhe is not aware of, just as you are not aware of what is in you.

But for now, you must continue to train your mind and your mouth to be silent. Not only in the woods, but everywhere you go you must put this into practice. This is important because you and Jim must be able to speak spirit to spirit. The less you speak, he slighter the chance of your adversaries hearing either of you or knowing your mind, your strategies. But for now, I must send you back. Jim is looking for you and he worries much. We will speak again for as AI said, I am always watching over you". And just like that, she was back on the stump and hearing jim running and calling her frantically. She shook her head and yelled so he would know where she was. "Gwennie, are you alright"? "Yes, I'm fine, Jim. What are yu doing here? I thought you and Ted were riding". "Well, yeh, we did. But I've been back for over two hours now". Seeing that she loked dazed, he asked, "How long have you been out here anyway"? "I'm not sure. What time it now"? "Gwennie, it's a little after seven now". "Well, as I remember, it was shortly after one when I decided to go for a walk. I felt like I need to work on that whole 'silencing my mind and mouth" thing, so I sat on the stump. But let's get I the house, and I'll tell you the rest, okay"? "Sure, my Gwennie. Are you sure you don't need me to carry you"? "Oh no thanks. I'm fine. Just stiff and I guess a few pinps and needles from sitting still for so long". By the time they entered the house, Gwennie was pretty much back to normal. Well, as normal as she could be. She was very hngry, so Jim ordered a couple of pizzas while she freshened up. Shortly after she came back into the den, the food arrived, so Jim went to the door to get it. "Here you are m'lady". "Two pizzas"? "Oh yeah, you must be out of it. I could eat at least one of hese babies by myself. And you said you really hungry, so two pizzas. Even though the way you eat, I'll bet you won't even eat half of one. Yu know my Gwennie, if I could hold an eating contest between you and a bird, I'll bet the bird would win". They both laughed. He said grace and they began to eat, quietly at first. Then Gwennie began to tell Jim all she could remember about her experience while she was I the woods. When she told hm that the angel had told her that she didn't know what was inside of her, Jim knew that her real identity was about to be revealed soon, certainly before they went into battle. They talked a while longr and by the time Jim left, his Gwenie seemed to be her old self again. Now that her training had begun, he knew she would never really be the Gwennie she used to be. That thought made him a little sad because he had loved his Gwennie just as she was for a long time. He never wanedwanted her ot change, bu change she must.

CHAPTER NINE

After Jim left, Gwennie disposed of the empty pizza boxes, smiling because she had certainly fooled Jim. She had eat4en siz large slices of pizza, surprising her own self. Jim congratulated her for finally having a "real appetite" for a change. They had both laughed at that. After making sure he den was neat again, she sat down at her computer, thinking she would do some writing then turn in early. Buta shar as she tried, the storyline just wouldn't flow. After half an hour, she gave up, thinking that maybe tomorrow would be a better day for writing. She decided to shower and get ready for bed, having an even earlier night than she had planned.

Nother dream. It was just another dream. Gwennie looked at the clock on her nightstand and saw it was barely midnight. She lay there, with her heart pounding and with breathing hard. This time she was in that place, what had the angel called it? She struggled to remember, and it finally came to her. The Elah Valley. The place where David had slqain Goliath. In the dream, she had been walking with the now familiar sword in her hand. She ha been trying to find Jim, but she dared not call him verbally. She knew they had to speak spirit to spirit, so that's ho wshe alled to him and that was how he answered. He wasn't in the valley, he had climbed up into the mountains and gave her directions to his exact location and in no time she was there with him. He spoke again in their special way and told her that the enemy ws already gathering hi forces. "For now, they're on the other side. But they'll be in place soon. For now, they can't see us, we are very well hidden from them. And as long as we communicate this way, they can't hear us either". When she again looked across the valley, it seemed that the number of "soldiers" had doubled. In the dream, her heart began to pound as though trying to beat its way out of her chest. Reading her, Dream Jim continued to speak spirit to spirit and said, "It's okay Gwennie. We can see them, but they cannot see or hear us. But you must conquer the fear you feel. In battle there are two things that can get you killed very quickly: fear and foolishness". "But there are only two of us. How can just two of us fight so mnany, and win yet"? "Remember what your angel told told you? He is always with you, as mine is always with me. There are many other angels watching over us, fighting for and with us. And yet others that minister to us. And there are messenger angels that will tell us things we need to know. So, no need for fear. We are fine and we will be fine". Suddenly, she was alone. Jim had disappeared. But wait a minute. Jim hadn't moved. She was the one moving. She was being transported, (the only word she could think of) from where she had been to somewhere else. Her heart was once again beating with a fierceness she had never known either in the dream world or th real world. She woke up before she found out where she was being transported to, and now she was sitting up in her bed wiping sweat ad trying to calm down her rapid nd hard heartbeat. Alooud she asked, "Why am I having dreams like this? At least I was used to dreaming about Jim and me walking through those dusty, empty towns. Why have my dreams change""? What she hadn't known was that even though Jim hadn't bveen asleep, his spirit had been in the dream with her. He had never experienced that before, but he knew that the connection he and his Gwennie had made it possible for such things to happen, especially when God was in it. He also knew the stronger their spiritual connection, the stronger their spirit-to-spirit communication would be and that would be extremely helpful to them in battle. He also knew that the dream was a part of her training, a part he himself could not take he through. It was necessary to help her grow bolder and more courageous, eve in the face of the unknown. He knew she would do well, once she realized what was happening. As long as he had known his Gwennie, she had never been one to run from anything she knew had to be done. She was a very steadfast person, and he reasoned that since this battle had to happen, he was glad to have her as his comrade. He trusted God above all and then he trusted his Gwennie as he had never in his long life trusted anyon else.

Once he was back in "reality", Jim sat for a minute, then went to get his ever-present cup of coffee. He very much wanted to talk to Gwennie, but it ws after midnight and he had always felt it was disrespectful to call or visit hr after ten p.m. Besides, he knew that if she needed to, she would call him. He knew she was awake; he could feel it. And he also knew that she was fearful and confused. He prayed a little prayer on her behalf, then picked up his bible and began to read. When he opened it, he saw 1 Samuel 17, the chapter about David killing his uncle, Goliath. After so many centuries, this was still a sore spot for Jim. He had come to realize that he couldn't couldn't change the past, and neither could he change what people thought about his family line, all because of his uncle Goliath. He had long ago accepted the fact that all he could do was live the best life he could, being kind and helpful to others. And this especially after coming ot know Jesus Christ, whucg was a challenge. When Mr. Beardsley had firt introduced him to God and His Son, hesus Christ, it had been extremely hard to believe that Jesus had died for anyone ine Godliath's blood line. As much of a good friend as Mr. Beardsley was to him, Jim had never confided in his friend as to his true identity. As a matter of fact, only Gwenie knew the whole truth about him. Even all the officials he dealt with when he first applied for social security card, driver's license and birth certificate. But there were always people in place to help hi. He thought some of those people probably thought e ad amnesia r some other mental disorder. Either way, God had provided all that he needed, not holding the wrong of Goliath against Jim. And for that, Jim was thankful. He looked at his grandfather clock and saw that it was nearly one o'clock Sunday morning. He thought about going to bed to try to sleep, but he knew he wasn't ready for hat yet. For some reason that "out of body" experience had left him a little wired; too much os to go to sleep anyway. Heturned his attention back to his bible and began again to read about David and Goliath.

At some point, he didn't know when, Jim had finally fallen asleep. When he woke up it was nearly ten on Sunday morning. He knew Gwennie would be getting ready for church, if she hadn't alreadyleft home. He grabbed the phone and quickly dialed her phone number. "Hello", a very sleepy Gwennie said. "Oh hey. Sounds like I woke you up, I'm so sorry". "It's okay Jim. How are you this morning"? "I'm good, thanks. I'm glad I got you before you left for church". "Oh, I don't think I'm not going to make it today. Rough night". "Dreams again"? "Yes. But again, different from the previous dreams. Friday night, my dream took place on the trail. Last night, I was back in the Elah Valley, and you were on the mountain. As a matter of fact, you ave direction to get up to where you were. You told me exactly where to place my feet with each step. Jim wanted so much to lt her know that he had experienced that "dream" with her but thought better of it. He would just listen to her. But as it turned out, there was no more to listen to because she yawned and told him that she was sorry, but she was really, really sleepy, which he understood. They quickly got off the phone and Jim thought he could stand to get some more sleep himself. He settled back in his recliner, but no matter how sleepy he felt, he just couldn't get back to sleep. After half an hour he decided to shower and dress, then make some breakfast for himself. Once all that was done, he'd eaten breakfast and cleaned his kitchen, he thought he would go to the bike shop for a little while, even though he found Sundays to be eerily quiet because he never allowed his crew to work on Sundays and the café was closed. It wasn't that Jim hadn't known quietness. Afer three hundred and forty-seven years of mostly being alone, he thought he probably knew quietness better than most people. But he thought the quietness at the shop on Sundays was heavier somehow, and he thought he knew why. On Monday through Saturday, there was aways huste and bustle, people aways in and out of the café and he and his crew were always clowning around while they worked. It was always good hearing those sounds all around to someone that had lived in so much silence.

After church Winnie and Ted decoded to have lunch while they were out, but neither of them knew where they wanted to go. Winnie said, "Well, we can always go to the café. Remember, we didn't take the leftover home last night. We can heat it up there or we can take it home. There;'s enough for both lunch and supper, if yu want it". "Well, for lunch is good, but I think I'll probably want something different for supper though". "That's fine with me. One does get a little tired of eating your own cooking". They both chuckled as Ted drove in the direction of the café. When they arrived, they weren't surprised to see Jim's bike in front of the shop. Ted unlocked the café door and went in to turn the lights on in the back, then helped Winnie take out the leftover food from the day before. Once it was loded in th car, he went over to speak to Jim. "Hello Jim. You doing alright today? Missed you at church today". Jim had been working on a bike repair, but his mind had been anywhere but there. He was thinking about Gwennie and her lessons. When he heard Ted's voice, he jumped up nd whirled around in one fluid like movement Ted was amazed at how quickly his big friend could move. A flash of Jim stopping the robbery fifteen years ago flashed through Tad's mind. He had no idea of Jim's age, but the man was fifteen yers older than he had been back then, and he still moved like lightening. "Oh hey Ted. How are you? How are ou and Winnie today"? "We're both good, thanks. We came by to pick up the leftovers from yesterday. You want to come to the house and have some lunch with us? You know you're welcome". "I appreciate that, man. But when I leave here, I plan to fo straight home". "Well, would you like us to make you a plate to take home with you? There's more than enough". "That's a tempting offer, but no thanks. I don't want to put you through any trouble". "No trouble at all. I'll be right back". Ted took the food back into the cafe and he and Winnie made three large plates for Jim to take home with him. The third plate was just in case he wanted to share some food with Gwennie. She was't in church either, so just in case she wasn't feeling well, she wouldn't have to worry about cooking, if she hadn't already. When Ted returned with the plates he said, "WE made three very ful plares my friend. Two for you and one for Gwennie just in case she's under the weather. I mean, we noticed she wasn't in church either". Jim sensing Ted and Winnie were really worried about his Gwennie, said, "Thanks Ted. And please thank Winnie as well. I'll take the plate to Gwennie, but she's not sick or anything. But anyway, what's the damage? How much do I owe you for all this food"? "Look Jim, you don't owe us anything. Truth is, without Win and me having ome help eating it, most of it would just be thrown away. We didn't get to make plats for the homeless shelter yesterday and their food has already been delivered for today. So, you see, you are doing us a favor by accepting it. All we ask Is that you and Gwennie enjoy it". "Thanks Ted. And you know we will enjoy every bit of it." Ted assured him that he was very welcome and said he's better get out of there before Winnie got tired of waiting for him and decided to leave him there. They both laughed and Jim said, "I can see her dragging you out before I can see her leaving you anywhere". As soon as Ted had gone, Jim called Gweennie to ask if he oculd bring the food over to her and told him that was fine if he could stay for a whle. He assured her that he could not stay but would be glad to do so.

Once they were on the way home, Winnie asked Ted if Jim had said anything about Gwennie an hwow she was doing. "Well, he did say that he isn't ick or anything. And that's all he said on that subject. Winwe have known for years that those two are close, but I never knew that Jim was so, well, protective wqhen it comes to Gwennie. So, in that light, I didn't ask any questions. I knew I wouldn't eget any answers anyway. But for some reason, I feel there is some secret between those two that he is protecting just as stringently as he protects his Gwennie". "Well, as you said before, it's none of our business, but I can't shake the feeling that something is up. Something, well, I don't know how to say it. All I know is that I believe those two need a whole lot of payers going up. Ted, you knowneiter of ushave ever been nosey people. I men we care about ffmily, neighbots and such, but we have never been like this before. And it's not just one of us, it's you and me both. I just feel, no I know, that something is either happening or wil happen. And I just want our friends to be oaky, you know"? "I kow, Win. We are on the same page. They do need a lot of prayer and I want them both to be okay too"". They were quiet until they got home and began to take th food into the house.

Gwennie's phone rane and thinking it was Jim, she said, "No my friend. I don't need you to bring anything else with you". But it was Delia on the other end. With laughter she said, "Well, I guess I got the answer to my question anyway. After I didn't see you in church, I wanted to see if you were okay and if you would like me to bring yu anything. But let me guess. Your friend Jim is on his way over". Gwennie laughed. "First, I'm okay. And thanks for checking on me. I was just so tired this morning that I overslept. By the time I got ready, it would have been too late to come anyway. And to answer your second question, yes, Jim is bringing dinner over to me". "Okay. For the umpteenth time, I'm being nosey. Are you sure the two of you are just friends, because you both act like yu are more than that? I know, I know. I alredy told you that I'm being nosey again. And yes, I already know what else you are going to say. You are going to sy that you are just really good friends. But looks to me like oe o both of you are living in denial". "Delia". "I'm just saying, okay? Anywy, since you are okay, I'm going to have my own dinner and watch a good movie on television". As soon as the word "television" was out, Gwennie couldn't help thinking about Jim's story about him see it for the first time and she couldn't stop herself from laughing.

"What's so funny about that"? "I'm sorry, Delia. It's not about. what you said exactly. You just reminded me of something, that all". "Oh, oky. Well, can we have lunch one day this week"? "Sure, jst let me kow. And thanks again for checking on me". "No problem". Just as the call ended Gwennie heard Jim pulling up into her driveway and went to open the door for him. "Come on in the house, Big Fella". Jim replied, "I believe I'll do just that", and entered with the basket of food that Ted had left with him earlier. He set the basket on the kitchen counter, then said, "I think Ted and Winnie thought the were feeding n army". They both laughed as he went to wash his hands. When he came back into the kitchen, Gwennie I appreciate all this good the food, but I thought they always gave the leftovers to the homeless shelter. Wonder why they didn't do that this time"? "Ted said they just forgot to do that. They had been so buy an were just plain tired by the time they closed I guess. I offered t pay for the is food, but he said they would have had to discad it if they didn't have someone to help et it up". "Well, I'll have to call Gwennie nd thank them for this. And Lord kows, I really did not have any intentions of cooking, so this is really right on time". "I hear you".

Before Delia could decide what, she wanted for diner, Lynn called to invite her to do out for dinner. Her husband, a construction worker, ha been working out of town for three months and could only make it home every other week. Lynn said this was the odd week and she didn't want to eat alone. Hoping to tempt Delia, she said, "Girl, I just felt like cooking, so I messed around and cooked too much. I can put some in the freezer, but it's nothing like having someone else enjoy your cooking while it's hot and fresh. I cooked roast beef with potatoes, carrots and pearl onions. I cooked collard greens, corn on the cob. I made corn muffins and two sweet potato pies. Then I this morning I decided to make some potato salad and now I'm getting ready to fry your favorite fish, whitings. So, how about it? Wan to come and help me eat up some of this food"? "Girl say no more. I am there. What can I bring"? "Nothing but your appetite". "And I cam sure o that. Now I'm kind of glad Gwennie couldn't go out to eat with me today". "Is she okay? I know she wasn't at church. I was planning to call hjer next and cheek n her and see if he wanted to join us for dinner". "She's okay. She overslept this morning. But there is no need to call her about dinner. Big Jim was on his way over there with some food". "Hmm. I wonder why those two don't just go ahead and admit that there is much more to their relationship than they say. Lord knows, neither of them can say, well, never mind. I don't want to gossip". "Okay. But what were you going to say though"? "It's just that it's like there is some supernatural bond between them"? "Supernatural"? "Yes. I can't explain it any bettr than that, other than to say it's like their individual destinies blendinto one destiny. I don't know. But I don't think either of them could find anyone else to love them and treat them any better". "I know, right? But, it's their business. Anyway, are you sure I can't bring anything with me? Want me to bring juice or soda or anything like that"? "Nope. Got that covered too. Unless you want a specific drink, butI made my favorite drink". In unison they both said, "Fruit punch Kool aid", and started laughing. "I should be there in about twenty minutes". "Alright, see you then and be careful". Will do".

"Oh man, I am so full! I know I ate too much, but Ted and Winnie's food is always so good". "Yes, it is. I think I ate a little too much myself. I fel like I can barely move". They had indeed eaten a lot. They had eaten roast beef and gravy, meat loaf, roasted chicken, mashed potatoes (and potato salad), mixed greens, sweet potato casserole, corn muffins and apple pie. Gwennie had only had a little bit of each food, but Jim had a much bigger appetite, so he really had put away quite a bit. They were finally able to go into the den, but they both sat in companionable silence for a few minutes. Gwennie started to nod off, so Jim told her he would leave so she could get some sleep. "I'm sorry, my friend. I'm just so sleepy today. But please don't leave yet. Unless you have something to do. Even if I were to go to sleep now, I wouldn't be able to sleep tonight. And I don't have any urge to do any writing". "Okay, my Gwennie. Whatever you want me to do. But I am surprised that the storyline isn't flowing, I guess. I know this has been a heavy weekend, information wise. And I know you are having prophetic dreams. I'm sue that adds to the heaviness". She looked at him with tears welling up in her eyes. "Gwennie, you know yu can always talk to me, about this. About anything. I'm always here for you". "I do know that, Jim. It's just that I don't really know how to explain the drem I had last night. It was so intense, and so, um, surreal. And now, hours later, it still feels as though I was inside the dream. I feel like I was there. I know it sounds crazy. But Jim, I'm not crazy. I just don't have adequate words to explain it". Jim was fighting to hold back the ears. It broke his heart to see his dear Gwennie in this state. He moved over to the love seat, put his arm around her shoulders and that was all the invitation she needed to let the tears come as they may. After she'd had a good cry, he grabbed a tissue and wiped her face dry. "Gwennie, you are not crazy. Listen to me, okay. You were there. In spirit. I know you have heard of out of body experiences, right"? "Yes". "Well, that's wat happened to you. I know, because I was here too." Thoughtfully, Gwennie said, "So, it's not just a dream". "No, my dear, it isn't. I didn't want to get into this today, but it's all a part of your training. Right now, you are going through the spiritual and mental preparation". "Why have you can I been chosen for this"?

"We were born f this. It's who we are. It's what we are". "Wait. You and I are from two different worlds and times though". "In the Spirit, that doesn't matter.

You've said yourself that we are all created with purpose and destiny. Your destiny and mine are intwined into one. That's why I had to come into the café when I did fifteen years ago. You were there and we were destined to meet that day, at that time. But I didn't know the attempted robbery would happen beforehand though. But when the robbers came in, I knew I had to protect you at all costs. My presence there was all about you my Gwennie". He sat quietly for a couple of minutes to give her time to absorb what he had just told her. After those few minutes, Gwennie said, "So, that's why you and I are so close, and why it seems like we know ac other so well. Even from the beginning of our friendship, it's been that way". "yes". "Did you know all of this at that time"? "I knew our destinies were one, but I didn't know how they would unite. I only knew then as I know now that you are very important to me. And that you always will be important to me, my Gwennie"". He choked up a little as he said that, and for the first time ever, se saw that he was blushing. "Jim, we have always been totally honest with each other, right"? He hesitated, thinking he didn't want to lie to her. He had never been totally honest about his feelings for her. He knew that for what they had to do together, they needed complete and total honesty and trust between them. "No, my Gwennie. I am so sorry, but I have not been completely honest with you for over twelve years now". He thought it strange that she didn't seem to be the least bit surprised. "Why aren't you surprised at hearing that"? "You never direcxtly told me that you arein love with me. I knew you were trying to hide that for whatever the reason. But your actions, and other words you say and the way you say them told me. It shows in the way you are ready to dro everything to get to me if I need you. And you know what, ZI have been just as dishonest with you. Because I know that I am in love with you too. I guess, no, I know that I have been afraid of my feelings. That's not about you though. It's just that when you have been hurt, it's so hard to love and trust again. I never told you, but long ago I was married. I was seventeen and he was nineteen. His name was Calvin. Calvin Leon Conklin. He was six feet two, muscular and his skin was the color of dark caramel candy. He had naturally wavy hair and he was the finest boy I had ever seen. We met at a basketball gme. I was a cheerleader and his younger brother, DeReno, played on the basketball team. One night, DeReno introduced us, and it started from there. My parents didn't like him at all, even though he appeared to vbe very respectful and polite. He attended the community college and worked at a local furniture factory. I had a part-time job at the local A&P. Anyeay, every chance we got we would date in secret hoping my parents wouldn't find out, but they did. I never knew how they found out, but they grounded me for one month. I couldn't drive or walk to school and work alone. They drove every where I need to go. After the month was up, Calvin and I started right back seeing each other in secret. My parents found out again, but that time they said they wouldn't try to stop me anymore because they saw was determined to date "that hoodlum". I couldn't see that in Calvin. I only saw a hardworking and studious young man who treated me well". She was quiet for a while and just whne Jim was about to say something, she spoke. "After I graduated high school, we wanted to get married, but my parents wouldn't hear of it. So, we eloped. Both sets of parents were very unhappy about that, sgreeing that we were too young, and that e should have at least finished college first. But for my parents, even wore was that their dislike of him had continued to grow. But they still l et us live with them until we could afford our own little apartment. My parents didn't want me to leave, still not trusting Calvin even though he had behaved perfectly well all the while we lived with them. He offered to pay rent, but they wouldn't hear of it. But he did buy groceries for him and me, telling my parents that although he appreciated al tey were doing for us, it was his responsibility to take care of me. I was so proud of him, but my parents still didn't trust him. Anyway, as I said, after six months we were able to move into our own place. We didn't have very much as money was tight, with both of us being in college. But my parens were kind enough to continue paying for my education, whch helped tremendously. And his parents helped as much s they would. But with three other boys to get through high school and college, they didn't have a lot of money to spare". Here she stopped her story nd told Jim she neede some water, which he told her he would gladly get for her. After a few swallows, she picked up on her story again. "Well, for a little over a year, we were a pretty happy young couple. Calvin would lose his temper occasionally, but e would just as soon calm down and apologize, so I didn't really think anything of it. I mean he'd never hit me or anything, so I thought we'd be fine". She took a deep breath and another drink of water. "Then came the day I found out I was pregnant. I was stunned and I knew Calvin would be as well. I mean, I trusted my birth control device to prevent an unplanned pregnancy". Now tears began to roll down hr cheeks, so Jim took her hand in his. When I told Calvin about the baby, he didn't just get angry; he went into a rage. He ws yelling and throwing things around. Ge accused me of sleeping around, and said the baby wasn't his. He was the only one I had ever been with before or after marriage. Then he started repeating, "No baby. No baby. No baby". He dropped down to the floor and curled up in the fetl position while he repeated it. Then, all ofa sudden, he jumped up and came over to where I was. He grabbed me by the collar and threw me across the room. I almost passed out. He began punching andkicking me, still chanting "no baby". It was onl by the grace of God that a neighbor was home and heard the commotion and called the police. By the time they got there, I was unconscious. But apparently, he wouldn't open the door and the police had to kick it in. When they did, he lunged at them and they had to tackle him. Somehow, he was able to get up and was attempting to run away when one of the officers shot him in the leg. I was out of it when all that was going on. When I regained consciousness, I was in the hospital with tubes attached all over me. I had two broken ribs, a a twisted knee and a sprained wrist. I was full of bruised and i ws swollen from my head down to my knees. All that and it turned out I had never been pregnant; the test had been wrong". Jearing all this, James "Big Jim" Beardsley felt an anger in him that he had never known before. He couldn't ever remember wanting to kill anyone, but he wanted to at that moment. With his mind's eye, he could see all that his Gwennie was telling him and he also felt all the pain she still carried within her. "Once I was well eough to talk to the police, they told me that Calvin had been addicted to steroids. That's why he ws so muscular. He first started using in his senior year in high school. He had been on the football team and had wanted to "bulk up", so a "friend" had turned him on to the "roids". I went into counseling even before I left the hospital and continued for over a year. But I still occasionally have nightmares about that nigt. He'd been in jail three months when it's said that he picked a fight with the wrong guy and though they couldn't proveit, the police thought that guy had smothered Calvin in his sleep. His parents never wanted to face the fact tht he had been an addict. They blamed me for everything. They told anyone who would listen that he had been doing very well until he met me. Then I supposedly made it worse by getting pregnant, but they never acknowledged tht the test the docor had done gave wrong results. Some year later, before he died, Calvin's father did come to me and apologize for all that had happened. He even admitted that they had seen signs that something was wrong with Calvin even before we got married. But they put it down to him being tired, what with going to school and working. I forgave him and a few months later he was dead. I cried because I had really come to love his parents. But Calvin's mother has never forgiven me. Last year, DeReno was home visiting her and we ran into each other and decided to have luch. So many years had gone by and I had never known that Mr's Conklin had also blamed him for all that happened with Calvin. She blamed him because he had been the one to introduce Calvin and me. He said that she is so full of unforgiveness, so bitter, that he hates to even visit her. And his other two brothers only visited once a year, but wouldn't spend a ight in the house with her. He only does it because she is his mother and he wants to honor her in any way he can because that's what God wants and expects of him. He said it would be good if he could move her in with his family, but he just can't let her spread her poison in his home, especially to his three underaged children. You know, it's sad that she hates me so much that she is treating her own son that way. So, you see Jim, my fear has nothing to do with you. I don't care about your size, your age or the fact that you are from Goliath's family line. You know for yourself that I didn't know about you rue age or the Goliath thing until very recently anyway. I see you for who you are. I see your beautiful and loving heart for people, no matter who they are. And I especially see the love in your heart for me. And I don't take that for granted. And I trust you whole heartedly. That' something I never thought I would hear myself say to another man. So that truly makes you one of a kind, James "Big Jim" Beardsley+. But I don't think I'm ready to shift into a committed relationship yet. Not with all we are facing. So, can we just keep things on a friendship level until all this battle stuff is over"? "Absolutely. I agree with you. We need our focus nd energy directed on our preparation. And sas long as we know how we feel about one another, we are good". Then he asked her if he could mke himself some coffee. She laughed and asked him what took him so long", and at that they were both laughing.

Um, um, um. Lynn as my grandma used to say, "You put your foot in it". This food is so gooder than good. Or maybe I'm just o hungry". They both laughed. "Thank you, Delia. Let's say it's a little of both, how about that"? "We can do that". "You know, for some reason, I just can't get Gwennie off my mind and I don't know why. I mean, you said she is okay, right"? "She said she was okay. She was just tired I guess and overslept. And she was oky enough for Big Jim to come over and bring her dinner". "Yes, so you told me. You know, we've known her for what, twenty yers or more, but ifyou think about it, we really don't know a lot aobout her. I mean she is a great friend to have and I love her dearly. But she doesn't talk abot herelf very much. Not like you and I talk about ourselves". "Ae you tryng to say that you think our friend is hding something? If so, I can't see that". "Oh no. I don't think she has some deep, dark secret or anything like that. It's, well, it's like there is a sadness dep within her and she's afraid to trust anyone with it. I don't know. Maybe it's just me". "No, that part isn't just you. For years I have sensed a sadness in her. I have wanted to ask her about it, but I figured it's her business and if she wants to talk about it, she will. I will say this though. I am willing to betg you that some man has hurt h very badly". "Why do you say that"? "Think about it. We hve both been out with her when men have approached her. And what does she always do? She has always politely given them the cold shoulder. That's why it surprises me so much that she and Big Jim have had such a close friendship for all these years". "You know, I know they're close and all, but I wonder if maybe it's partially because she feels safe with him. Not only is he super big and super-fast, but he Is definitely protective of our Gwennie'. "This is true".

Ted and Winnie had finished sinner. Since lunch had been a big one, they decided to make a salad for dinner. As they sat eating, they talked about the menu plans for the week. They knew they couldn't take meatloaf off the list for the wa one of their most popular items, along with mashed potatoes, green beans and mixed greens. So they needed to figure out something they hadn't cooked for a ewhile. Ted said, "Tell me something, Win. Why do we plan menus months ahead, then go back and change them every week"? Winnie laughed. "Teddy, that's a very good question. All I can say is that the menus are never written in stone, you know. And don't forget. It's a woman's prerogative to change her mind", she said with a laugh. Ted shook his head and laughed. "Well, after thiry years, I guess I wouldn't have it any other way". "Me either, Teddy. Me either". She looked over at the kitchen counter at all the food that was still left. "I wish we had left more of that fod with Jim. He and Gennie could have frozen a lot ofit for later". "yeah, they could have. I guess I just wasn't thinking. Just like I was't thinking about getting the food to the hoeless shelter Friday. I really hate that. Speaking of which, I have an idea I want to ru by you. We need a bigger refrigerator at the café, right? So, what if we donate the old one to the shelter? That way they could accept mre donations each day instead of having to rotate the way they do now. Oh. By the waqy, I called Sal and she told me ot to worry about missing it Saturday. Appatently another restaurant has joined the circuit and had donated a "ton of food", as Sal put it. So, even more reasn for the to have an industrial refrigerator. So, what do you say? Are we in agreement on this"? "Sounds good to me. But we'll need to clean this one really well before taking it over there. I don't want Sal to have to worry about doing that. Poor old thing, her hands are aready full. If I had the time, I would love to volunteer to help her. Do you know that every tie she tried to ge funding there is always some excuse for not helping her. As a matter of fct, she told me tht if it wasn't for "that nice Mr. Beardsley", she would have to shut down the shelter. Sis you know that he has been paying the electric bill every month for the last five years"? "No, I didn't know that. But I'm not surprised though. Jim Is a very big-hearted guy". "He is. He also does a lot of repairs around there. Anything he can do to help Sal save money". Winnie chuckled. "What's so funny"? "Sal said she would love love to have him for a husband. But I don't see that happening. If that man marries anybody, it will be his Gwennie". "I agree with yu on that. I wonder has the subject ever come up between those two"? "I wonder that too. If they ever do decide to get married, that's one reception I would like to cater for free. There was always a sadness in each of them, but since they have become friends, it seems like it's been different. They have really been good for one another s far as I can see". "Yes, and I would love to either be the bet mn or give her away. Either way I'd be fine, just as long as I'm in that wedding". They agreed that they wanted that particular wedding to happen, and the thought made Winnie smile with anticipation of catering that reception.

Jim was hungry again, so he and Gwennie had gone back into the kitchen. Gwennie had always loved watching Jim eat. He always ate as though evry bite was a rare delicacy, savoring each bite. And he wasn't one of those messy eaters either, he was surprisingly neat. She ha always admired that about him, but it seemed that she admired it even more now. She wondered if the difference had been brought about by the freedom that came with finally being able to express their feelings for one another. And as Gwennie was doing her thinking, Jim was doing some thinking of his own. He couldn't believe how light and free he felt in finally being able to tell his Gwennie that he was in love with her. But what was comical was that she said he had been giving himself away the whole time he thought he's been hiding it. And she had loved and respected him enough to let him tell her in his own way and his own time. What a great lady. Acknowledging their feelings for one another made the world seem brighter and happier somehow. But he knew his Gwennie was right. It was best to leave their relationship as it was, at least until after they'd gotten through the battle. Of course, tha was no guarantee. They both just had to hope and pray that it was God's will for them to make it back alive. If he didn't make it, he thought that would be oaky. After three and fory-seven year of life, he had seen so much and done so much. But in comparison, Gwennie was just starting to live, even at the age of forty-seven. His main concern, his most pressing prayer need was for Gwennie to be kept safe before, through and after the ensuing battle. He reasoned that if he had to choose who would live and who would die, he would gladly die for his Gwennie. But what he really wanted was to have some more time with his love. Evn if he was "older than dirt", as his Gwennie teasingly called him. His Gwennie. Even those words had a new feel to them. It felt so good to be gfree to admit that his Gwennie was the holder of his heart, she had it under lock and key, and he always wanted it to stay that way. And he wanted her to always trust him with her heart. She had already had so much pain in her life, (he still felt a certain rage thinking f that). He wanted desperately to love that pain away, to bring more love, joy and peace than she had ever known.

Monday morning dawned bright and sunny. Gwennie stepped out onto her back porch and thought she had never seen the sun shine so brightly. The birds were singing so beautifully that she thought they could all line up a stage and give the greatest concert anyone could ever enjoy. The leaves on the trees looked greener than they eer had looked to her. And she felt lighter somehow. She felt a freedom that she had never felt nd couldn't explain to anyone. And she knew why she felt the way she did. It was because she and Jim had finally been fully honest with one another. They had finally proclaimed their love for one another, and that was the freedom she felt. She began to giggle as she thought, "I am in love with a three hundred and forty-seven-year-old man". She giggled like a sixteen-year-old who was talking for the first time to a boy she really liked. Then she said, "Lord, thank You. I never, ever thought I would feel this way again. But this time I feel it more richly, more deeply. Maybe it's because I'm much older now. But no matter. I just want to thank You for bringing Jim into my life". Just then her phone range. It was the lov of her ife. "Good morning, Jim. How are you on this glorious morning"? "I'm well, thanks, my Gwennie". She thought, "I have heard him call me that thousands of times over the years, but this time it has a richer sound and feeling than ever before. She couldn't stop herself from smiling. "What are your plans today, other than working on your new book, that is"? "That's about it, I think. I'm a little behind in reaching my goal. Why do you ask? You have something in mind"? "Oh. Well I was hoping we could meet at the café for lunch. But I know how much you like to stay on schedule with your books, so I don't want to disturb that". "Jim, yu are never a disturbance in any way. I can meet you if you like. What time do you want me to be there"? "Is one o'clock good? I have a customer coming in at noon, but I should be done by one". "Sure. Anyway, I guess I'd better let Winnie and Ted see for themselves that I'm not at death's door". They both laughed. Then he prayed over them and their day, and they said they would see each other at one.

"Well, look what the cat fragged in", Winnie exclaimed. She didn't think she had ever been happier t see anyone enter the café than she was to see Jim and his Gwennie walk in together. "Gwennie, I was beginning to wonder if you'd abandoned us". "Oh no, Winnie. There is no way I could abandon my friends and the best café in the whole wide world", she said laughingly, and everyone else laughed as well. "Well, have yourself a seat and I'll be over in just a minute to take your orders". "Sounds good", Jim said. Once they were seated, Jim said, "Well, I would say Winnie is one happy lady now that she sees that you really are alright. I have never seen her like that before". "It's a wonderful thing to know that we are loved", she said as she looked him eye to eye. And he whole heartedly agreed with her.

One of the waitresses had taken their drink orders and had served the thjeir iced etea. Then, true to her word, Winnie came over herself to take their order. "Okay, my friends, what will it be for you"? Gwennie ordered first. "I think today I want some of that food old meatloaf, new potatoes, green beans". Jim decided to have the roast beef with gravy, mashed potatoes, mixed greens and corn muffins. Once Winnie ha walked away Jim said, "You know, my Gwennie, we have had lunch together dozens of times over the years. But today feels so different. It feels really good in a very special way". Gwennie smiled and said, "I feel the same way. I was standing on my back porch the morning before you called. I was thinking how much brighter the sun seemd to be shining and how the songs of he birds seemed to have such harmony. And the grass and the leaves on the trees seem to be so vibrantly green. And you know what else? I am feeling a freedom that I have never felt before. And I know it's because for the first time in all do msny years we have been fully honest with one another". Winnie walked up with their food in time to overhear the last part of that statement but pretended not to hear. "Well, my dear friends. Here is your food, fresh and hot". "Umm", Gwennie said. "It smells so good and I know that like always, it will be just as delicious as all that food you sent yesterday. By the way, thank you and Ted for thinking of me as well as Jim. That was so thoughtful of you". "Oh, it was our pleasure. As I believe Teddy explained to you Jim, you two dd us a favor by accepting that food. So, we must thank you. Both of you. Okay now. Is there anything else I can get for you"? "Oh no thanks. I think we are good". "Well you know what to do if yo need anything. Enjoy".

Back in the office Winnie told Ted, "There is something different about those two". "What do you mean"? "I can't explain it exactly. It seems ike they are even closer somehow. It's the way they were looking at one another. Teddy, honestly, that look between those two reminds me of how we looked at one another when we firt fell in love. I don't think they are just friends any more". "Hm. Well Win, in all honesty, Jim has always behaved as though there was more than friendship. I believe that was love at first sight. If you can remember, think about how he looked at her when he first saw her. And think about how close they have been since that day. I mean, Jim has always been friendly and helpful and all, but there just wasn't a lot of joy and happiness. But once Gwennie came into his life, he has laughed a lot more and he even began to joke around some". He stopped and thought for a minute. "Yes, Win, those two are so goof for one another. And who knows, maybe we will be attending a wedding soon".

Jim and Gwennie ate quietly for a few minutes, enjoying their food. Suddenly Gwennie asked, "So are we still starting the training on Wednesday"? "Well, technically your training has already started, as I'm sure you know. You have already begun the spiritual and mental training. And now that we have been real with one another, we will be able to do more speaking spirit to spirit. We will reach a point where we will be doing more of that day by day because the more, we do that, the better oooour communication will be in our preparation and most assuredly during battle. The enemy won't be able to hear what we are saying to one another and that will cause a ot of confusion in their camp and we will have he element of surprise on our side". Gwennie leaned toward him and asked, "Jim, how do you know all this stuff? I mean, was it taught t you along the way? Or had God spoken to you and explained al this to you"? He looked steadily into her eyes, then said, "If I knew the answer to that, I promise you I would tell you. But I truly don't know how I know all of this. I just do. It's like something that was, I don't know, like it was somehow planted inside of me and s just now blossoming. That's the best way I can explain it". Gwennie thoughtfully nodded her head. "I guess I understand that. It's just that you are so confident in this. It just seems like you know everything that's coming even befe it does come. So, I thought surely you must have been through all this before". "As crazy as it sounds, sometimes it feels that way to me. But even though I can't remember everything I have experienced in all these years, I would remember something like this, I think". Out of the corner of his eye he saw one of the waitresses approaching and spirit to spirit said, we will have to finish this later" to which she responded, ""Gotcha". They were both astonished at how quickly she ahd received and responded. He had always known that his Gwennie was a fast lerner and was always proud of her. But in that moment, he thought he had never been prouder of her. She would surely do well in the heat of battle. And he was proud that his Gwennie was the one that had been chosen to fight by his side.

Gwennie had been back hone for a few hours and was dipinto her manuscript when her phone rang. Trying not to let her aggravation be heard on the other end, Gwennie took a deep breath and answered. "Hello". "Hey Girl. How are you today"? It was Lynn. "Hi Lynn. I'm good, thanks. How are you"? "I missed you at church yesterday. Later I wanted to invite you to dinner, but Delia told me you had other plans". "Yes. I'm sure she told you that Jim was bringing dinner over for me". "Yes, she did tell me that. I'm sure you enjoyed that, probably more than you would hve enjoyed dinner with us". "I did. I enjoyed it very much. But I still love you and Delia too". Lynn laughed and said, "I know you do. And I'm glad you did enjoy your dinner with Jim. But may I be a little nosey right now"? "Gwenie chuckled and responded, "Why are you asking permission? You're going to be money no matter what I say. So, what do you want to know"? "Wel, when are the two of you going to admit that you are more than just friends? It's obvious to anyone that sees the two of you together that you love one another". Gwennie smiled a huge smile. She imagined that if someone saw her now, hat smile would be all hey could see of her face. "Oh, so you think yo haveit all figured out, huh"? "Well, yeah. So, what is stopping you? I mean yes, he is bigger than big and maybe a little older than you are. But the guy is a sweetheart, especially where you are concerned". "Okay, now I have two questions. Why do you assume I am the reason for not saying we are more than friends? Maybe he doesn't want it that way, ever think of that"? "Girl please. Quit playing. What's your other question"? You were saying Jim mght be a little older, so how old do you think he is". "I don't know. Mid sixties maybe. Not a day over sixty-five, if that". It was all Gwennie could do to hold in the laughter. "Good answer. According to his driver's license, you are about right". They chatted a little while longer, then agreed they would have lunch together later in the week. After ending the call, Gwennie thought about Lynn's guess at Jim's age. She thought back to the time she had asked his age and she wondered why instead of answering, he had shown her his driver's license. At that time, his age was fifty-six, according to hi slicense. And she had figured he was a well preserved fifty-six. (At that time, she had no way to know just how well preserved he was). Now she knew the answer to that question. He hadn't wanted to tell her the truth, but he didn't want to her either. She looked at the picture she had of him on is bike. She had seen that fae at least a thousand times and had always enjoyed looking a it. Jim was one of those ruggedly handsome men. And Lynn was right. He really didn't lok a day over sixty-five. She thought about the Israelites and theit gotty years in the wilderness. Not even their clothes and shoes wore out, so she knew God could and would preserve. But Jim was a three hundred and forty-seven year old man that looked like he was only sixty-five, The man could move like lightening and was unbelievably strong. If she hadn't believed in miracles, knowing the truth about Jim would make her believer. She chuckled as she thought how so many people, if they only knew the truth, would love to find out how Jim had stayed so young for so many years. She would like to know that herself. But she figured that was between the Lord and Jim.

What Gwennie didn't know was that Jim had asked the Lord many questions along those lines himself. Not getting the answers to those questions, he decided that it was God's business an ot his own. But with the ensuing battle, he felt that his time was almost up. He hed he was wrong about that. For so many years, it didn't really bother him to think of leaving this world for the next. He was alone and had been for far too long, s he felt he had no real reason to want to stay. But then he met his Gwennie. And he began to feel things he had never felt before. And those feelings made him want thigs he had never wanted. Now, he found himself asking God isf it was His I will, would he grant him many more yars with his Gwennie. He knew it was all up to God, but he figured he would make his request known just the

CHAPTER TEN

Promptly at ten, Jim had called his Gwennie to pray and say good night. But this time there was one difference. This time he had been free to say, "I love you my Gwennie", just before saying goo night. And she had been free to say those words right back to him. He thought he had never heard a seeter sound in his whole life. When he fell asleep a little late, he still heard her saying those sweet, beautiful words to him.

At midnight, Gwennie decided it was time to shut it down for the night. The words were coming more and more lsowly now, and that was always her sign to stop working and get osme rest, or at least to do something else for a while. She brushed her teeth and washed her face before changing for bed. She hadn't realized how tired she was until she was finally stretched out in her bed. She remembered that she hadn't knelt and prayed. "Lord, I kow I didn't physically bow down tonight. And I know that You are paying more attention to my heart, than the position of my body. I could actually kneel and still mt reverence You as You deserve. But

Lord, YoOu know I love You and I am so grateful for the way You love me, keep me and provide for me. And oh God, forgive me for anything I may have thought, said or done that displeased You. I do want to please You. And sas usual, I ask You to continue to bless Jim, but this time I ask it as more than a friend. Lord, it's obvious that You love hm and that he is quite special to You. I mean, You have kept Him as only You can for all these years. And You have preserved him even better than You preserved the Israelites, so in my mind that confirms that he is quite special to You. Okay, It's official Lord. I'm rambling. But how do I pray for him? I could at least have some idea of how to pray before. But now that I know the truth about him, I truly don't know how to pray. But then you did say in Your word that we don't know how to pray and what to pray for. So, Lord all I know is to ask You to please keep doing what You have be been doing for over three hundred years, okay"? Before she could get any other words out, she fell asleep.

Jim was a little tired and a lot sleepy, but he couldn't settle himself to make it into dreamland. He finally got up and went to sit in his recliner to read for a while. He picked up his bible and when he opened it, he saw Psalm forty-six, "God is our refuge and strength, a very present help in trouble". He thought about what he and his Gwennie had coming. They certainly hd their share of trouble coming, that was for sure. And only God could bring them through it. He looked at the grandfather clock and saw that it was now shortly after midnight. Tuesday had already come in so they had only one more day before the physical part of Gwennie's training would begin. They decided to start on Wednesday at five p.m. The thought of that made him think of the "Swords of Truth" he had to teach her how to use. He had found those swords over one hundred years ago. He couldn't remember exsacty when and where. In all his walking and in all those years, most of the tiem he never knew where he was anyway. All he could remember was that at some point in his travels, he'd seen the box. He remembered that he was walking across a desert and had gotten tired, and he had been very thirsty. He sat down on a huge boulder and closed his eyes for a very short time. He knew he hadn't been praying, he hadn't learned to do that yet. When he opened his eyes, he looked around and saw nothin but sand and more sand. Suddenly, out of the corner of his left eye, he saw something ont eh ground beside th boulder. There was a wineskin lying thee beside a long dark, half rotted wooden box. He remembered asking, "Now where did this come from? I know it wasn't here before". He had picked up the wineskin and found it was very cool to the touch. He opened it very carefully and found sweet, cool, lifesaving water in it. He had wondered again how it had suddenly appeared but gave no second thought about drinking any of it. He wanted so desperately to dring it all down at that moment, but he also knew that he didn't know when he would find fresh water again, so he only took four or five swallows. But even that small amount of water had revived him. And even after all these years, it still amazed him how that water had lasted until he got to another town, Upon leaving a town, he would refill the wineskin and the water was always cool and fresh and it never ran out. He thought that one day he would have to share that part of his story with his Gwennie.

Then he had concentrated on the wooden box. When he opened it, he found a long black cloth bag inside. He carefully pulled it out of the box and found inside two uniquely made golden swords. Around them was a note written on papyrus. In Hebrew were the words, "The Swords of Truth". It is the destiny of you and one other to become one with each other and with these swords. If you believe, you will be guided by the Truth. Take care of these swords, for your responsibility is great now. Yahweh be with you." Even aftr all those years, the note was still in the same condition in which he had found it. And so was the carry bag that the swords were in. Jim had never once hd to shine up the swords, nor they never lost their glow and neither had they lost their edge. Over the years he had often wondered who "the other" would be; where and when would he meet him. Jim had never even entertained the thought that it would be a woman. But then came the day that he met his Gwennie. H'd been working in his shop when he's felt that by then, familiar electrical pulse course through him. He had told his crew that he would be back nd immediately gone next door to the café. When he walked in his eyes had immediately met Gwennie's and he thought she wa the most beautiful lady he had ever seen, and he ahd known that she was the reason he'd had to be thre. Then he two would be robber came in and Jim had sprung into actn. He was glad that it was good for everyone there, but all he could think of was saving the beautiful lady he had bveen destined to meet. That day brought into his life a joy he had never known. He knew that day that he was in love with her and would do anything for her.

His thoughts turned back to the swords. "I guess I'd better get tehm out soon. I think by nex week we will be ready to train with them". He thought about Gwennie's question, wondering how he knew all that he knows about this whole battle thing. He had told her the truth. He had asked himself that question many times but had never gotten an answer. He had come to believe that it was another one of tose things that was God's business, and the answers would come only when He was ready to give them. He finally felt himself getting sleepy enough to get some sleep, so he thought he would get into bed and whispered a prayer for his Gwennie, the love of his life.

While Jim was lost in his reverie of thoughts, Gwennie was in dreamland. This time she had started out walking the trail behind her house. She came to the stump that now seemed to be a key part of both her waking life and her dreams. She sat down and listened to the bird sing their beautiful songs. Each sang a different song, yet they all blended into one melodious sound. Suddenly she heard footsteps on the path nd turned to look in the direction from which the sound came. Facing the back of her house, dream Gwennie became concerned that someone mght be trying ot blocvk her from getting back to it. She stood up, not even aware tht she had taken a fighter's stance, with her walking stick ready for action. The footteps slowly continued to come towards her, but she stood her ground, alert, but unafraid. The footsteps stopped just about five feet from where she stood. Suddenly drem Gwennie said with confidence, "Psalm ninety-one says He who dwells in the shelter of the Most High will abide in the shadow of the Almighty. So, I am not afraid of you". She needn't have made that last statement, for as she quoted the scripture, she heard the footsteps run away from her. Sream Gwenie turned and continued her walk, thanking the Holy Spirit for speaking through her, or at least telling her what ot say. Suddenly, she wasn't on the path amy more, but was in the Valley of Elah. This tiem here was no angel and neither was Jim there. It appeared to her that she ws all lone, but he didn't feel like she was alone. She wasn't afraid, she felt a certain peace and strength envelope her. As she stood there looking around, she herd/felt a voice saying, "You have pssed the test. Your enemy attempted to frighten you and force you to turn bqack, to run away from your destiny. But you stood your ground and used the

Sword of Truth on him, so he hd no choice but t run away. You have passed the test and you may rest now". And rest well she did. She slept until her phone rang at eight that morning. It waqs Jim, making his usual good morning call so they could pray together. "You sound like I woke you up, my Gwennie". "Hi Love". They were both a little surprised that she had called him that, but it had felt good, even right to both of them. "You did, but I'm glad you did. I should have been up an hour ago". "Did you have trouble sleeping last night? Any dreams"? "Yes, I did have a dream", and she proceeded to tell him all about it. "And after I heard that I'd passed the test and that I was to rest well, there was no more dreaming. I just slept, rather soundly I think". As she told Jim about the dream and what was said to her, he thought, "I am not surprised that my Gwennie passed the test. And Lord I thank You for allowing her to get some good sleep. Thank You". He's said those last two words aloud without realizing it. "What are you thanking me for"? Quickly Jim said, "For just being you". And soon after they ended their cal with their "I love you's and talk laters".

Gwennie lay in her bed for a few minutes, thinking about he r life. Afte all she had gone through with Calvin; she had never intended to let any other man into her life. She just didn't thik he rhart could stand being so torn apart again. In he rmind he knew that not all men were like him, but he just didn't ever want to take the chance to find out what man was or what man wasn't. She just did not want to expend time, effort and energy in all that. She had her parents, who had moved to Florida after retiring. They talked twice a week and they visited each other four times a year; her going to tehm twice and they coming to her twice. She had her writing, her friends and her hobbies. But most of all, she had God. And that had been enough for her, until James, Big Jim" Beardsley had come into her life. She had to admit that she loved the change, she loved him. Her big "Mountain Man" had definitely brought a lot of joy into her life, and she wouldn't have it any other way. But it still blew her mind that she was in love with a three hundred forty-seven-year-old man". She giggled as she headed to the bathroom to shower and dress for the day.

When Gwennie arrived at Neenah's Restaurant, she found that both Lynn and Delia were waiting for her. When she approached the table, Lynn said, "Well, the gang's all here. How is our Gwennie today"? "Hello my girls. I am well. How are you two today"? Delia said, "I'm offended. I ask you to join me for a meal and you turn me down to e with your Jim. But Lynn calls and here you are. I'll tell you; I have got to get some new friens". They all laughed. Once the waitress had taken their drink orders, Lynn said to Gwennie, "I really was concerned about you Sunday. It's not like you to miss church without something being wrong". "Thanks Lynn. But as I told you both, I ws just so tired and sleepy Sunday morning that I couldn't get myself up and dressed in time for church. I wasn' sick or anything, just tired". "Well, I'm just glad you are okay". Delia said, "Well, there is one thing about it. If something was to ever be wrong with you, we know that Big Jim's got you. That's for sure". Things got quiet very quickly and Delia said, "Oh Gwennie. You know I always pick on you aboub your Big Jim, and you always have some comeback waiting for me. Why so quiet now"? "Oh no, Delia. You know good and well that I don't pay any attention to you. I suddenly thought of something pertaining to my new book. So, believe it or not, your teasing came in handy for once". They all chuckled at that, then picked up their menus to decide on what they each wanted to eat.

As they ate, they shared with each other what had been happening in their lives since they'd last met. Gwennie was very careful to avoid sharing anything that had taken place with her and Jim. Not that there was anything to be ashamed of, but it was as her mother always said, "Don't serve up your business on a silver platter". So, she mostly stuck to talking about ideas for "Please Don't Pass the Sugar". Normally she didn't discuss the details of a new book, but at that moment she felt it was safer to talk about that than to let the conversation linger too long on the subject of he rand Hm. She could sense that both ladies' curiosity abo0ut that subject had heightened. Not only were they curious about her relationship with Jim, but about the man himself. They only knew what pretty much everyone in town knew; that he owned a bike shop and was exceptionally gifted at customizing bikes. They had even herd that a fe of his bikes had sold for over a million dollars. Of coure, Gwennie always knew how much one of his custom bikes sold for, but when asked, her response was always the same; "You have to ask Jim about his personal business". So finally, Dekia and Lynn had stopped asking questions about James "Big Jim" Beardsley. They found Gwennie to be as close mouthed about him as she was about her past. But their curiosity was so heavy that it fet almost tangible. Finally, sensing that Gwennie was being exceptionally careful to avoid the subject of Jim, Delia asked if there were any deep, dark secrets she ws hiding about Big Jim Beardsley. In surprise, Gwennie asked, "Why would you ask a question like that"? "Oh, I just want to know if he is, in secret, a bank robber or something. Or if he is some "masked avenger" type". Gwennie chuckled and said, "If he were anything like that, I think I would know. No, Jim is just, well, Jim. Big hearted, caring and loving Jim". "Now that I get. I have heard more than once that he has single handedly funded more than a few programs for the elderly, kids, and the disabled". "Um-hm", Delia said. "And according to Sal, he is the reason she has been able to keep the homeless shelter going. Apparently, he pays the electric bill evey monh and makes any repairs he can so Sal can save money. Quiet a "friend" you have there Gwennie. But I'm sure you already know all this". It was Lynn that finally changed the subject, and for that Gwennie was truly thankful. "You know, I wonder why the city and state don't give Sal moe help in keeping that shelter going". "Well, at the Admin building, it's said that she doesn't eget much because there aren't "enough" homeless people in this area, so the bulk of the money go to the larger cities. The city dies what it can to help, but there is just not enough money to go around. They have to fund the senior citizen/disabled person programs, as well as the programs for special needs children". "I understand that, but it's a shame it's l;ike that. I wish I could do mor to help Sal, especially during the winter. I mean I donate a few groceries when I can, and a few blankest, socks and what have you to help", Lynn said. "I do too, Whatever I an do, when I can do it. And whenever I get any kind of bonus at work, I donate a little money, but that's still not enough. And I think it's great the way some of the restaurants joined together to take cooked food over there each day". "Gwennie was quiet, and it didn't fo unnoticed. "Gwennie, are you sure you're, okay? You are awfully quiet today". said Lynn. "Oh yes, I'm fine. You two just reminded me os something I was supposed to have been doing to help Sal. My parents had left a couple of boxes of clothes behind for me to take o the shelter the last time they were here. I feel bad because I don't know how ZI could have forgotten to take them to her. Maybe because I'm not in my guest room that much. But like you guys, I do what I can to help Sal too. I really worry about her though, because as she gets older, I see it's getting harder for her to keep things going. I'm glad that at least Community Service will send teenagers to help occasionally. And I'm sure any help her friend Millie gives her is a blessing to her". Gwennie hadn't lied when she's said she had remembered that he needed to deliver some clothes to the shelter. She had also been thinking about the kindness of her Jim. Of course, she had known about a lot of his goo deeds, but he hadn't mentioned that he had been paying the electric bill for th shelter for all those years. But then, that was Jim. He was a very meek and humble man who never "tooted his own horn". He just loved people and hated so much to see anyone suffering in any way, whether he knew them or not. Whatever he did for anyone in any way was truly from his big, loving and giving heart. Gwennie was unaware that a mile had come to her faceas she thought of her Jim. Delia said, "Gwennie, I'll bet we can guess where your mind is. With that big smile, you are thinking of Big Jim, aren't you"? "As a matter of fact, I was thinking of him, and how proud I am to have that big man in my ife". Neither Delia nor Lynn missed the glow that was on her face. They both now knew for sure that there was more between their precious friend Gwennie and her" friend" Jim. What they saw on her face was nothing less than pure, unadulterated love. Se could deny it all she wanted to, but that ldy was in love, just as he was with her. Lynn and Deia glanced at one another but chose to say nothing about what they had seen. They went non to talk about other things until it was time to leave the restaurant.

While Gwennie was lunching with Delia and Lynn, Him was working feverishly to finish customizing a 1968 Harley Sportster he had been working on. He hadn't decided whether he would sell this one or ride it himself. He had alrdady gad two offers for it even though it wasn't finished. One offer was from a rider from Texas who had been traveling through. He and his family had stopped at the café to get something to eat, and he noticed Jim's Custom Bikes right next door. The man had told Jim that he ahd a collection of vintage motorcycles and would love to add that particular bike to his collection. He had heard of Jim and his work and was glad to finally neet the man himself. He said he had even seen a couple of bikes Jim had customiszed and was quie impressed. He had also told Jim that "The Lord works in mysterious way. I have been wanting to meest you and shake your hand and here we are. I was looking gor another restaurant, but m wife wante us to try the one next door. If they had continued traveling North on 220, they never woud have seen either building. But when they saw the Ted and Winnie's Café sign, the decided to take the side road. They had talked for a bit, then one of the vacationer's sons came over to tell him he needed to come on so they could order their food. Jim had wondered what it would have been like to hear his own son say something like that to him. He was a living witness, a walking testimonial that God could do anything. But he just didn't think kids would be in his future at his very advanced age. Still, he had found himself wondering what it might have been like for him nd his Gennie to have had a child together. Would it have been a son who would have taken after his father and grew up to me a huge man? Or would it have been a dainty little gitl who would have been his own little China doll? Oh well, wondering about that was all he could ever do. Still, it ws nice to do even that. He gathered his thoughts and got back to work on the bike. He wanted to finish it because once he and Gwennie begasn their training, he didn't think it would be long before they would find themselves in the battle of thir ives. She stood up, stepped back and thought, "I think I'll kee this one. I want my Gwennie to ride with e at least once on this one. Yep, not selling you old girl", he said as he stroked the bike lovingly.

Once Gwennie was back at home, she decides dshe'd better walk the trail for a little bit. She had eaten a lot for lunch, and she thought she'd better walk it off before she sat down to work on the book. She changed into her hiking boots and grabbed her walking tick on her way out the back door. At the head of the path, she remembered her most recent dream and began to retire Psalm ninety-one. She didn't feel any fear, but still, she figured it never hurt to spek theword. If nothing else, she figured God would like that, and He was the main One to [please. When she came to the stump, she sat down and thought it was a good time to practice silencing her mind and her mouth. And she thought she would try speaking with Jim spirit to spirit, just to see if she could do it. She sat still and silent, for how long she didn't know. After a while, she thought she was ready to try to speak to Jim. She took a deep breath, then, thought, "Hey Jim. Can you hearme"? Jim was so surprised that he almost dropped the bike part he was holding. Gwennie! I hear you clearly. Are you okay"? "Oh yes. I came out for a walk and thought I would just try this to see if I could do it". "Well Babe, you did it. An all on your on. I really am proud of you. I really am". "Thank you, my Love,". Suddenly the conversation ended, and she was fully back on the path. For an instant, she wondered if she had really talked to Jim, but then she knew with surety that she had really connected with the love of her life. She started back toward her house and suddenly she saw a shiny copper coored snake in the middle of the path. She stopped and looked directly at it. The snake actually seemed to look directly into her eyes and she thou9ght, "It's trying to mesmerize me". The it started to rise as though it was growing feet. Suddenly she thought about Exodus 7 and how aaqron threw down his staff. It became a snake. Pharoah's magicians did the same and their staffs beame snakes too. But Aaron had God on his side, so his snake ate up the magcians' snakes. So, without thinking about it, Gwennie threw down the walking stick, staff, if you will, and said, "In the name of the Lord". She couldn't believe what she was seeing. As in the bible, her walking stick became a snake and it surely did devour the other snake, then turned baqck into a walking stick. "Wow. Lord, I have never experienced things like You have me experiencing here lately. I don't know why You have chosen me for all of this, but I just don't want to let You, or Jim, down". She hesitated to pick up her walking stick, but suddenly she heard Jim say, "Show no fear. It's only your walking stick. The enemy knows we are soon to fo into battle and he lso know that you are a much stronger, more courageous and fiercer warrior than he thought you would be. He underestimated you, my dear Gwennie. You passe the test, and I am so proud of you". "So, you never left me? I mean, you were here all the time. Did you know that smake would appear"? "Here, yes. But no, I didn't know about the snake itself. I just felt that something would happen, so I kept the doorway between us open". "I'm glad, but it woud have been nice if you had warned me that something was going to happen". "Then you wouldn't have passed that particular est. Everything is good now. I'll call you later. I love you, my Gwennie". "Okay. I love you too". Then there was complete silence as Gwennie walked back to her house.

At the exact moment the snake showed up on the path, Winner felt a sudden urge to pray for Gwennie, and so did Delia and Lynn. It wasn't as though there was any conversation between them that led to this for the were all in separate places. Delia was on her job at the city administration building. Lynn was at the hospital prepping a patient for surgery. And of course, Winnie was busy at the café. All three whispered prayers for their friend's safety as they wondered what was going on wih their precious friend. Anjd all three of them thought there was one thin for sure. If she was in any danger and Big Jim Beardsley could get to her, she would be alright. Delia thought, "That big, strong, lightning-fast man man loves himself some Gwennie. So, if he is nay where close to her, he'll make sure she's alright. No doubt about that". None of the ladies had any way of knowin what was going on, ut they felt certain that Gwennie was, r would be, alright. And like Delia, they thought if Jim was close to her, he would make sure she was alright. Just as Winnie finished that thought, Jim walked into the café, and for asecond or two, Winnie looked at him in surprise. "Win, what's wrong with you? Why ae youlooking like that"? He was looking in the same direction she was looking in and saw Jim walking in. "Win"? "Oh, nothing, Teddy. Nothing at all". ButTed, who knew his wife quite well, knew better. He knew something caused her o look at their friend with that surprised look. But he would have to wait until they were alone to get that out of her. He turned his attention to Jim as t big man seatd himself at the counter, where he always sat when he was alone. It was only when he was with Gwennie that

BIG JIM

he sat at a table. "Jim, how are you, Buddy"? "Oh, I reckon I' good for an old man". "I hear you". Ted heard him but had no idea just how old he "old man" really was. "So, what can I get for you today"? Jim decided to have a light lunch of three fried chicken breasts, mixed greens, macaroni and cheee, corn muffins and a slice of lemon meringue pie. A full course lunch for anyone else, aligh snack for Big Jim. When his platte was ready, he paid his bill and was heading back to his shop when Winnie stopped him and asked him to come back to the counter for a minute, which he did. "Jim, is Gwennie really alright"? Surprised, Jim responded, "Yes she is, Winnie. Why do you ask"? "You might think this sounds crazy, but a little while ago, I had, oh, an unction I guess, to pray for her, and to pray urgently, for her. It felt like she was in danger". Jim instantly knew what that had been about but didn't want to tell Winnie about the "test". "Well, thanks for praying for my Gwennie, Winnie. But she's alrght. And Winnie, having an unction to pray is never crazy. Thanks again and I'll let Gwennie know that yo0u were thinking of her and praying for her.

As Winnie and Jim had their conversation, Gwennie was at her computer working on her book. Like Jim, she felt she needed to finish he book as soon as she possible\y could. She knew it was because of the preparation for, and the upcoming battle itsef. She had no idea something ike that would last. And neither did she know if she would survive something like that.

Physically, she had onl ever been in one fight. And tht had been on the neighborhood playground whe a little boy pushed her down. She ha blacked his eye in return. Spiritually, she had only thought of prayer as battling with the enemy. Ntil now, she had never even dreamed f herself being involved in something like this. She had heard of prayer warriors, and what some called demonologists, but she had never thought of herself as either of those. She turned her mind back to her manuscript and soon the storyline was flowing quite rapidly. Within te minutes, she was lost in her characters' world.

    As Jim sat eating his late lunch, he thought about Winnie's question about his Gwennie. From what the lady was saying, she had to have been led to pray for Gwennie around the time the snake had appeared on the path. So now he wondered if Winnie was assigned as an intercessor for Gwennie, or for both at this time. And if that was so, could Ted be assigned too? He had initially thought they were being a little nosey about his Gwennie, but maybe there was more to their questions, their concern. And the good Lord knew that he and Gwennie would need all the sincere prayer they could get, because the battle would be fierce, even potentially deadly. He decided he would talk with his Gwennie about it. That way they could pray together about that specific thing and make the decision from there as to whether they should let Winnie and Ted in on what was going on. He had no way to know that Delia and

Lynn were also connected somehow, but it wouldn't be ong before he would find out.

Once they had closed and their employees were busy cleaning the café, Ted and Winne were in the kitchen working alone, which finally gave him the opportunity to ask Winnie the question he had been wanting to ask all afternoon. "Okay Win. What was it all about. Why did you look so surprised when Jim walked in here earlier? It's not like he doen't come in here often or anything like that. So, why the surprise"? "Teddy, I really can't explain it. You know how we can get sudden functions to pray for someone"? "Yeah, I do". "Well, I had one of those earlier today, just before Jim walked in. I was surprised because ZI had the feeling tht he was with her. That feeling was so strong that if I were a betting woman, I would have put a pile of money on it. That's how strongly I felt it. But unless she was over at his shop, he couldn't have been with her. I don't know eddy. I just know something is going on with those two, and I don't think I am just being nosey either. And why did I feel so strongly that he was with her when I had to pray for her, urgently I might add".

Delia had been on pins and needles to talk to Gennie and see if she was okay. She also wanted ot talk to Lynn to find out if she'd had a strong urgency to pray for their Gwennie like she did. She knew Lynn was working until seven thirty, so she wanted to give her time to get home and get settled. She wanted to know if it had hit Lynn at about the same time it hit her to pray urgently for Gwennie. It wasn't as thought that had been the first tiem she hd ben led to pray for someone. Vut it was a rare thing for her ot be led to pray with such a forceful urgency. She also wanted to ask Lynn anther question if she had experienced the same thing. She wanted to know if Lynn had felt strongly that Big Jim had been with Gwennie at that time and that he would protect her. At that moment Deli wondered why that last even mattered. She had the feeling that something was going on with those two, and it wasn't just their relationship status either. Delia felt that something heavy was either happening or about to happen. And it would involve both Gwennie and Big Jim. She didn't know how she knew that other than it had to be the Holy Spirit letting her know it. It had to be Him. Her imagination wasn't strong enough to think up something like the things she was thinking and feeling. Just then her phone rang, and it was Lynn. "Hey Girl. I have been waiting to call you. How are you"? "I'm pretty good", Lynn answered, sounding as though she was trying to figure if she was giving the right answer. "You sound like you're not too sure about that. Something up"? "Well, around three o'clock I had this, prompting I guess, to pray for Gwennie. I mean, that thing hit me strongly, but I couldn't call to see if she was alright because I was prepping the last patient for surgery. I have been led to pray for others like that, but not as strongly nor as urgently. And you know what else? For some reason I felt that she and Jim were together abd would take good care of her. As much as he was able to anyway. I mean we know he's not God, but we know he isn't going to sit back and let any harm come to his Gwennie". As Lynn talked, Delia was wondering if she was having a dream. Everything Lynn said was almost identical to her experience, even the time it had happened. "Lynn, I experienced that very same thing at the same time. This is just too crazy. But I'll tell you this. There is something going on with those two. I have never ben prophetic or anything, but I know that either something major is happening with those two, or it's going to hppen. We just need to keep praying for them. That's all I know about all of this. And I think I will call Gwennie when you and I get off the phone". "Well, I just got off the phone with her. She says she is just fine, and she did sound like it. At least until I asked her if anything happened to her around three o'clock. She did begin to sound a bit strange then. Her answer was that something happened, but it wasn't anything major and again said she was just fine. When I asked if Jim had been around o help her when "whatever it was" happened, she responded, "Not exactly". But before I could ask what that meant, she changedThe subject, sounding like her old self again". "Hmm. I wonder what that does mean. Either he was with her or not. I really don't think he would ever do anything to hurt her, but then, I haven't always been the best judge oc men's character either". That last statement triggered memories of her own painful past, dating back to when she was eight years old. Of course, at that age she couldn't pick and choose who was to be in her life. But by the time she could make that decision for herself, she hadn't chosen well at all. For all tho years she ha believed that she didn't deserve to be loved and to be treated well. She had taken so many beatings over the years that without realizing it she had come to think of herself as nothing but someone's punching bag, and that was all she eve would be. But st the age of twenty-nine, she learned that one man had loved her enough to die for her. At first it was hard to wrap her mind around that. Men didn't die for you, they onl abused you. No, no man had died for her, that was just a made-up fairy tale. But two days after her twenty-ninth birthday, she was trying to figure out how to break up with her then present "fist-o-matic". She had grown weary of life with all I's abuses; physical, verbal, mental and emotional. She had just started her jb at the city administration building. She became friends with Sarah, the woman she shared an office with. One day Sarah had asked Delia to go with her to lunch, saying she really needed to talk abot something. So Delia had obliged her. Once they were out of the parking ot Sarah said, "I got out and you can too". "What? Got ot of what"? "The same thing you are going through. It was harder for me because I was married to my abuser, and we had two children together. I had considered suicide, thinking that death was my only way out. And one night, after e of he "vad" beatings, I looked at myself in the bathroom mirror. But instead of trying to patch up my injuries, I grabbed a bottle of pills in the medicine cabinet. I didn't even look to see what they were. I just opened the bottle and dumped the pills into my hand. Just as I lifted my hand to my mouth, I felt something, a hand, grip my wrist and force me to dump the pills down the sink. Something, someone had hold of my wrist, but no one was there. Then, and I know all of this sounds crazy, but I plainly heard "Get out. You were not created to be treated this way. Jesus died for you because of His love for you, not so you could be abused. Take your boys and follow me. Pack only what you and your sons really need and follow me. If you do as I say, all will be well. But if you don't, if you stay, you will die prematurely. And it will be soon. Now come with me and don't look baack". So, as I was directions, I did what I was told. I didn't know where I was going, and I only had three dollars and some change. But I was desperate, so I trusted someone I couldn't even see to help me take my sons and get out of that abusive situation. And by the grace of God, I haven't looked back. I got my divorce. My husband had disappeared by that time, so I had no problem with that. I later found out that he had died from alcohol poisoning. He had died in some back alley out in Fresno, California. His girlfriend had reported him missing and one of her friends found hs body. But my point in this is that if you trust God to help you, you can get out safely too.

I will help you. If you have nowhere else to go, you can come ;veith me while you get yourself together. My sons are grown and ive with their own families, so I'm there alone and I would love th company". So, Delia had taken Sarah up on that offer and hadn't loke back. And it was through Sarah that Deliea had learned of God's love for her and to that very moment, Delia had never been able to thank Sarah enough.

"Delia, are you there? Are you listening"? "I'm sorry, Lynn. I suddenly took a trip down memory lane. What wee you saying"? "I was saying I just don't think there is any way Jim would ever do anything ot hurt our Gwennie. He loves her too mch. And well, I just don't thik anything evil is in the man. Think about it. We have heard stories of people strying to start fighs with him because of his size and he always walked away. And we know he didn't walk away out of fear". "That's true. And I feel the same way. The only way I believe he would hurt or kill anybody would be if they tried to hurt his Gwennie. Hey how did we get on this subject anyway"?

"It started out with both of us thinking he may have been with Gwennie when she went through "whatever it was" that he went through earlier". "Oh yeah. Well, I think I will give her a quick call. I'll feel better if I hear her voice for myself. I'll talk to you later and have a good night". "Thanks, you too".

With phone call after phone call coming in, Gwennie figured she had best put down her writing for a while anyway. She loved her friends, and she knew they loved her, but she just couldn't understand why they were suddenly so worried abot her. Well, okay, maybe she could understand just a little. When you ar suddenly prompted to pray for someone, you will be concerned for that person or group fo people, or whatever the case may be. But both Delia and Lynn sounded like they were more than a little concerned, they sounded worried. And from what they both said, they were both led to pray at about the time that strange looking snake showed on th path, trying to both frighten her and block her from her house. The thought of that snake brought back to mind something she had seen it do. That snake had turned itshed to stare at her, but its body stayes stretched out across the path. It ws a demonic thing. Anda spooky thing. Her mind turned back to her conversatons with Lynn and Delia. Only the Holy Spirit could have led them to pray for her at that time, and she was grateful. But now she wondered if they might be somehow involved in the upcoming battle. Could they be assigned intercessors for her and Jim? Oh well. When she and he talked she would talk to him about that. If not tonight, then tomorrow when they started the physical part of their training. Speaking of which, she wondered just what that training entailed. Did it mean that she had to learn to move as swiftly as Jim did? She thought about his superhuman strength and dismissed that thought. In her earlier dreams shay had seen herself and Jim carry peculiar looking swords, they had crosses on the handle. And in the dreams, she had to admit that she thought she handled hers well. But that was in the dream. She really hoped she would learn all she needed to know and that she would learn well and quickly. As far as she knew she and Jim were the only two in this on their team, so there was no room for error. Two links didn't make a chain but still would be harder to pull apart, as long as each link remained strong and true.

Jim had gotten home a little later than he had intended to. He'd meant to be home by six, call Gwennie and see if she felt like having dinner together so they could have a much needed conversation, especially with training starting the very next day. But as he was preparing to leave the shop, he'd had two business calls come in back-to-back. Both had been customers he ha ddone work for in the past. They were both so pleased with his previous customizations that they wanted him to now do other bikes for them. He had gotten details the details he needed from each of them. He would later call them with the estimates of what the jobs would cost. From the details they had each given, neither job would be complicated so they shouldn't be very time consuming and shouldn't cost more than a few thousand dollars. Still, he wouldn't be able to five a definite quote until he could inspect the bikes to see what the starting condition woud be. If there were dents and dings to straighten out, the job would naturally cost more. He looked forward to working these projects and a part of him wanted to stay at the shop and begin working on the estimates for each job. Nut a greater part of him knew he needed to get home. It was past eight, so there aas no way he would ask Gwennie if they could have inner together. By the time he got home an got cleaned up, it woud be about nine-thirty, and knowing that they had a ful day ahead of them, he just couldn't and wouldn't do that to her. So, instead he would go home, get cleaned up, have a bite of supper and then call his Gwenie as he always did. Mayb they could plan to et together even earlier tomorrow afternoon so they could have a good heart t heart before the training began. He quickly showered, and made a light supper of bacon, eggs and toast. And of course, his ever-present cup of coffee was hs beverage. Once he'd finished eating and the kitchen his dishes washed, he was ready to make his nigtlycall to his beloved Gwennie.

"Well, hello my love. How has your evening been"? My love. Everytime Jim heard Gwennie call him that it seemed he fell even more deeply in loe with her. "Oh, it's been a good one, thanks. Just when I was ready to leave the shop, I had two formr customers call, back-to-back. They each want me to do another job for them. Sao, how about yours, after the path incident, I mean"? "It's been okay. But there is something I want to talk to you about. Are you very tired? If so, we don't have to talk about it right now". "Gwennie, tired or not, if it's something you want to talk about, then let's talk.

Bedsides, there is something I want to talk to you about as well". "Okay, if you are sure. Just do me a favor first, okay"? "Sure. What is it"? "Make sure you have your coffee". They both laughed. "I'm ahead of you, Sweetheart. I've got it right here. So, what's on your mind"? "Well, something a little strange happened this evening. The short version isthis: both Delia and Lnn called me to see if I'm okay. Nothing strange about that, we all check on each other fairly often. What is strane though, is that they were both prompted to pray for me at about the time the snake appeared on the path. And even stranger was the fact they both said they'd felt like you were with me and that you wee taking care of me, no matter hat was wrong. Jim, you and I both know you weren't with me physically, but you were with me spiritually. It's just strange that they felt that. I mean know the Lord works in mysterious ways, but, I don't know. Am I crazy? Or dould they be tied to this thing? Do yu think they have been assigned to intercede for us"? "No, my Gwennie, you are not crazy. And I o believe that they are somehow a poart of this. As well as Winnie". "Winnie? What do you mean"? "She was also prompted to pray for you at about that time", then he went onto tell Gwennie about Winnie's reaction when he's wa;ked into the afe, and the conversation he's ha with the lady just before he left the café". "So, what do we do? Do we share with them what's going on and what's about to happen? Or do we stay quiet about it"? "I don't know for sure my

Gwennie, but just for now, I think we'll just need to stay quiet. If we need to tell them anything, I believe God will let us know that. But for now, I really don't want any distractions while you are in training. It's going to take all your concentration to learn all you need ot know as it is. If we talk to these lhose ladies right now, I fear they will hae too many questions. And I'm not saying they can't be trusted, but they may be talking to someone and let something slip. And that we just cannot have". "I'm good with that". They went on to make their plans for the following day. They would meet for lunch at Ted and Winnie's. Afterwards, they would spend one hour walking either at the park or the trail behind Gwennie's house. At the end of that hour, they would begin the lessons with more work on silencing the mind and the mouth, to help their focus. Then on to the the spirit-to-spirit communication. By the end of that, one would think it would be an easy, more leisurely afternoon. But Jim knew that it would be anything but that. He didn't know how or when he had learned all the things he knew; he had certainly never been involved in anything like this before. All he knew was that the good Lord had kept him around for a mighty long tiem and had kept him in excellent health, and more and more, he reckoned this was why. He started to think about how in three hundred and forty-seven years, he couldn't remember a really sick day. Of course, as he'd been growing older and older, there were days that his energy level wasn't quite up to par. And he's had a few colds now and again. At that moment he began to wonder what doctors would think if they'd ever had to treat him for anything. And if one ever had to perform surgery, he guessed they really would want to use him as a test subject. But by God's grace and mercy, none of that had never happened. His strength had never failed him when he really neded it most. His appetite had never waned and as far as eh knew, he ha always been about the same weight since adulthood. Of course, he couldn't be sure of that, but he reckoned he couldn't be off by too much on that. But all that aside, God had been the One to preserve him for so long, he thought the battle was the reason, and Jim just wanted to show his thanks by not letting God or his Gwenie down.

Knowing that Wednesday would e a full day, Gwennie thought it best to shut down the computer early and try to get some sleep. Instead of a shower, she opted for a long, hot bubble bath, thinking it might help her get to sleep more quickly. Now, as she sat in her garde tub, she thought about what was laying ahead of her. Once again, she found herelf asking God if He was sure it was her that He wanted in this thing with Jim. Only once had she gotten an answer and even then, it had been only one word; "Yes". No explanation had followed, so she decided she would leave it alone, hooping that God would at a later time give her the answers she sought. Either way, she had been chosen for what was lying in wait for her and Jim. She thought about Jim saying that he didn't know how he knew all the things he did know regarding the training in preparation for the upcoming battle. She knew Jim waasn't a man to lie. God, bad or ugly, he was always one to tell the truth. So, she knew he really didn't know how he knew, but it appeared as though he did know. One would think he had been through this multiple times by the way he always knew what the next steps should be and how they should be executed. Well, on thing about that. She trusted God and she trusted Jim. Suddenly a question came front and center in her remind, flashing like a small-town caution light. She knew that this was a spiritual thing, but could their natural bodies die in this battle? If not, why all the physical training? She thought she must remember to ask Jim about that. She finally decided to fet out of the tub and get dressed for bed. She thought she was relaxed and sleepy enough to go to sleep now. But once she was in bed, she found she still couldn't get to sleep. She began t o have her nightly conversation with her heavenly Father, thinking, "I should have been doing that anyway. "Lord, forgive me please. Nomatter how sleepy, I my first priority should have been to spend time conversing with You, not trying to get to sleep". Finally, she did fall asleep and almost immediately began to dream. She saw the shiny copper colored snake again. This time it had attempted to stand on its tail as it spoke to her and that's when she noticed I wasn't the same snake. This one wasn't quite as shiny or as long.

It had said, "You are no match for me. Why don't you surrender now and save yourself from the ravages of the battle. You will only die anyway. Accept the fact that you cannot defeat me". Gwennie had pulled out the sword she had carried in so many dreaqms and said, "You know, you are right. I'm no match fr you". The snake had actually smiled an eery, evil smile at her as it still tried to stand on its tail. "On my own, I am no match for you. But I'm not alone. Greater is He who dwells in me, than he that's in the world", she said as she swung the sword and cut the snake's head off. Dream Gwennie was suddenly in one of the dead, dry towns that she and Jim had walked through. She turned a corner and suddenly there stood Jim, but he was diddrent somehow. He seemed to be even taller and bigger somehow. So much so that she had to hold her head way back to look up at him. "Jim, why are you so much bigger now"? "I'm not bigger Gwennie. Your perception is changing. All the food thins will seem bigger to you and all the evil things will seem smaller to you. With God you can defeat the evil and see it as nothing to fear. Therefore, it's not as significant to you as the things of God are. Remember: Greater is He that's in you than he that's in the world". "Wow". Ijust told that snake that same thing". It was at this point that she realized that they had held a whole conversation spirit to spirit, and she had been the one to initiate it. They were got quiet, even in their spirits, and walked, swords ready for the enemy. About fifty feet ahead of them to their left was now a shuffling sound in one of the rundown buildings. Dream Jim had moved to the left of dream Gwennie, sword drawn and ready for business. His spirit told her spirit to walk immediately behind him, back to baqck and have her sword ready. There was no worry abou that last part, she'd had it ready anyway. Even in the dream she found it amazing that step for step, they were in unison. EEven though she was walking backwards, she never faltered. They moved together so fluidly that had they been the same size, one would have thought they were the same. Suddenly, a snarling mangy don was running toward her, foaming at the mouth. And there were two of them running at Jim. Thye both had their swords raised and in unison said, "In the name of the Lord", and in sync, swung their swords, taking the heads off the hell hounds, Jim cutting off two heads at once. So, in sync wee they that their voices, though different, sounded as though they were one. They resumed their walk through the town, not even speaking spirit to spirit. Suddenly Gwennie felt herself being jerked and life away from Jim and that town. She was now on the trail behind her house and hearing someone tell her, "It's time to wake up now", and she sat up in her bed, sweating and panting, as her heart beat out its own quick rhythm in her hcest.

Jim woke woke up with a start. Gwennie thought he always knew what to do, by the hadn' seen that dream coming. In her earlier dreams of walking through the town or towns, only dream Jim had been there. But this time, he had been there with her. And he found it just as amazing as she did, the way they had moved so fluidly together, even though they were back-to-back. They flowed and even spoke as one. In that moment, in the dream anyway, they really had been one. But what concerned Jim the most was the way She had suddenly been taken away. It was though someone or something had jerked her violently to get her out of there. Now, he was worried, wondering just what that could mean. She had told him of being jerked away when they had been on the mountain overlooking the Valley of Elah, and he remembered that as well He looked at the clock and saw that it was shortly after three, but he knew he would never get back to sleep. He washed his face and hands, then went into the kitchen to make a fresh pot of coffee, still wondering why his Gwennie had been jerked away from him in the dream. Once he had his cup of coffee, he went into his den and sat in his recliner. He didn't want to have the television on nd he didn't want to read either, not even the bible. Without realizing it, he began to talk s though he was having a conversation as though speaking to someone who was in the room with him. Of course, no human erson was there, but he knew Who was. He knew God was always with him and was always listening. But what he needed even more than Him listening, was for Him to give Jim some qanswers. "Okay, so what was that all about? Why was my Gwennie snatched out of that dream? This is the second time it has happened. Are yo telling me that you are going to take her away from me in some way? I don't feel like she was dying or going to die. It felt like she was jerked out of the dream to save her life. Lord, would You pease just let me know what that is about. And is she asks me what it's about, how do I answer that"? Thinking of his beloved Gwennie, he knew her well enough to know that she had a heed full of questions as well.

Gwennie sat still in her bed, waiting for her heart to stop it fast pounding. She finally reached over to get eh bottle of water on the nightstand. After a few swallows, she began to feel a little calmer. She thought about how first there had been another snake, then eh dos that she couldonl think of as hell hounds. IN the dream she hadn't felt any fear, none at all. Shen her focus went back to the way she and Jim had moved and spoken as one. Even in a dream, where one could do pretty much anything, that had been nothing short of amazing. Aloud, she said, "Wow. That was wild. Just might hve to use that in a book at some point". Then she remembered that once again she had been snatched out of the dream. "Why? What in the world does that mean? It doesn't feel as though I am dying. It's more like someone or something is saving my life". She took a few more sips of water, then laid back down. She remembered the previous dream in which she had been snatched out of. Jim had been there that time as well. Oh, how she really wanted to talk to him. She felt that he was awake, that he ahd experienced what she had experienced, but just in case she was wrong, she didn't want to risk waking him up this early in the morning. She closed her eyes, took a coupe of deep breaths, exhaling slowly.

When she woke up again, it was almost seven thirty. Gwennie didn't know what time it was when she had finally gotten back to sleep. All she knew was that while she hadn't had any more dreams, the little sleep she had gotten was restless. She felt tired but figured that was nothing a nice hot shower couldn't fix. She sighed and threw the covers back so she wouldn't yield to the temptation of trying to go back to sleep. Just as she stood up to go into the bathroom, her phone rang. Knowing it was her Jim, she answered, "Good morning my "mountain man". How are you this morning"? "Hello my Gwennie. It sounds like I am a little better this morning than you are. You sound like you need to go back to sleep. Is the dream bothering you"? She didn't know why she was so reprised that he knew about the dream. They were there together, at least until she got snatched out of it. "Yes. It is bothering me, but we can talk about that later. How are you this morning, really". "I'm good. I think I know what you really want to know, but as you sai, we can talk about all that later". "Jim, would you mind very much if I changed our plans for lunch"? "No, but what do you have in mind"? "Well, how about I make us some lunch here? I don't know why, but I just don't want to talk around anyone. You okay with that"? "I'm good with it, but instead of you making anything, why don't I bring lunch with me? I'll cll you later and you can just tell me what you want". "Sounds good". They then prayed together which was their daily habit and ended the call.

By the time Terd woke p, Winnie was already deep into her morning devotions. He could tell from the position of her head that she was praying. They usually did that together, but he knew that his Winnie had a lot on her mind. And he knew it centered around their friends Gwennie and Jim. And he had to admit that he too felt a great concern for those two. Initially, he'd thought that maybe he and Winnie were hsfd tskn a turn onto the nosey side, even though that had never been either of them. But very quickly it had stopped feeling like nosiness and grew into a deep, troubling concern. And it had all started that day that Gwennie and Jim had left the café, looking, and behaving very differently than they normally had before. But now, especially after the episode that Winnie experienced yesterday, he knew it was something definitely wrong with those two. Something detrimental. He knew that by the time he showered and dressed Winni would be in the kitchen cooking breakfast, so he began to pray as he went about his morning's preparations for the day.

Winnie had eased out of bed shortly after four o'clock. She had looked over to make sure that she hadn't disturbed her sleeping husband of over thirty years. He was still peacefully sleeping with his usual light snoring. She went into the guest bsathroom to shower and dress for the day, and after that she went into the kitchen to put on the coffee. They had the electric coffee maker, but Ted preferred his coffee perked the old-fashioned way, on top of the stove. And she had o admit that she loved the smell of it going all through the house. She then went into the den and turned on some soft instrumental worship music and knelt down to pray. She began with her adoration of God the heavenly Father. Then she began to thank Him for His greatness, His grace and mercy, and on she went. Before long though, she began to pay fervently for Gwennie and Jim. She prayed in the prayer language, knowing that she had no clue as to what she should pray or how to pray. All she knew was that her heart was heavily burdened for her friends. She had not realized that she was crying until she ws ready to get up and get breakfast going. She went into the bathroom t wash her face and hands and went into the kitchen, where she found Ted prepating to cook. "Good morning my sweetheart. You beat me out of bed this morning. You okay"? "Good morning, Honey. I am good. I just felt that I needed to go into prayer earlier than usual." He could see that she had been crying but chose to not mention it. He would wait until she was ready to ell him what it was about, although he felt he already knew. She continued, "I had a dream last night, a disturbing dream. But I can't remember the details ofit, only that I know it disturbed me. You know, I think it may have even frightened me a nit". Ted was thoughtfully quiet for a few seconds, then said, "Winnie, I'm starting to think that maybe weare to intercede for Gwennie nd Jim like never before. I haven't had the unction to pray as you have had and I haven't had any dreams or anything, but I feel it strongly. Something is happening or will happen to thoe two and I believe ever what that thing is will be life changing. Neither of ehm will ever be the same". "I believe that too, Teddy. I believe that too".

Delia was usually one of those people that liked to stay I bed until the very last minute. For years now she had deliverately set her alarm fifteen minute earlier than the time she would get up. After hitting the snooze two or three times, she was usually redy to start her day. But this morning, she had awakened. Screaming, from a bad dream. When she had looked at her clock, she had seen that it was barely five thirty. She sat up in her bed and closed her eyes, trying to remember all the details of the dream. Gwennie and Jim were in the dream, and they were in danger. She had tried to warn them of something, but neither of them had even known she was there, much less hearing her cries for them to watch out. And tThat was as much as she could remember. Knowing she would not get back to sleep, she finally got out of bed, knelt down and prayed, then went into the bathroom to shower and get ready for her day. Since she was ready one and a half hours early, she thought she would make herself a full breakfast. And with that decision made, she found that she really was hungrier than she usually was at that time of morning. She made for herself scrambled eggs nd cheese and bacon. Not being one to make homemade biscuits and not wanting toast, she opened a can of biscuits, whichshe would have with butter and grape jelly. Not too healthy, her doctor would say, but it wasn't as though she did this very often. When the food was all ready, she sat down and enjoooyed it. "Not a bad meal for someone who haes cooking", she said to the empty room. She go tp, put everything away and washed her dishes and headed off to work. All the while, she hd still been thinking of the dream she's had and wondered if it was really telling her something or if she'd had it because she had been worrying about her friend, Gwennie. She couldn't tell, but she did know one thing. That dream frightened her.

Lynn's husband, Harold entered the kitchen where Lynn was making breakfast and said in concern, "Good morning, Beautiful. How are you this morning"? "Good morning Handsome. I'm good. How are you"? "I'm good. So, what in the world were you dreaming about early this morning"? "Why do you ask"? "It was like you were trying to warn someone of something. You were mostly muttering, but I did hear you sy "watch out", and something about "behind you". Did you look at some horror movie before coming to bed"? "Oh no. No horror movies for me. You know that very well", she said as she tried to laugh it off. "No, I don't really remember what I dreamed; I just know it was a frightening dream. And I know that Gwennie and her friend Jim were in it. I think they were in danger". "Oh. Well, maybe you should call Gwennie later to make sure she's okay then". "I will". They went on to talk about what they had to do that day. Lynn, as usual, would be preppig patients for surgery. Since Harold was home for two days, he would make use of that time by making small repairs around the house and he promised to cook dinner so Lynn wouldn't hav to worry about it. Thanking him, she kissed him and was out the door, heading to work.

Gwennie had made three attempts at writing, but the storyline just didn't seem to want to flow. All she could do was sit there staring at the screen, thinking about all the dreams and strange occurrences that had, of late, but invading her life. Even when she was young, she had begun to believe that everyone had a purpose and a destiny. And for years she had believed that it was all wrapped up in her writing. She believed that as long as she had accepted Jesus as her Lord and Savior, as long as she did her best to serve God with all her heart, everything would always unfold and work out the way He wanted it to. (She had long go learned to surrender to God's will and way). But she never once thought al this could have been a part of her purpose, her destiny. She wondered again, wh her? She saw nothing special about herself that would make he rright for this "job". But he also knw that as long as God said do it, she would, even if she didn't understand it. Just then her phone rang. It was Jim calling to see what she wanted for lunch. They decided on pizza and garden salad. He would pick up the food and be there in about an hour.

CHAPTER ELEVEN

Once they had finished with their lunch, Jim and Gwennie hit the trail behind her house. Neither was saying vry much, for each was lost in their own thoughts. Gwennie was wondering what this part of her training entailed and praying she would e able to learn well and quickly. Jim was praying that he would hear/feel clearly what he was to teach her and that he would teach his Gwennie all she needed to know, as she needed to know it.

Upon reaching the stump that had become Gwennie's trail seat by now she sat down out of habit. "Tired"? She chuckled. "No. I guess it's habit now to sit here. This is where I began learning ow to silence my mind and my mout, learning how to focus". Jim squatted down next to her and said, "Well, this is as good a place as any, I guess. Are you trady"? "My love, I'm about as ready as I will ever be, so let's do it". "Alright. From this moment on, we only talk spirit to spirit. To this point you have been trained to focus while sitting still. Today, you begin learning while walking. The more you learn to focus, the sharper your senses become. You will learn to sense movement before you see or hear it. You have done well so far in not showing fear when anything unexpected has been thrown at you. But now you must learn to focus and function even in the midst of a bunch of clatter. So, as we walk, I will make various noises. And your mind must be trained to simply react to what is there without wondering what something is or how to handle it. You must learn to recognize the difference between sounds and feelings of real danger and when there is no danger. So, you won't know what noises I will make o when. But I will warn you that at some point, there will be another test. Even I don't know when or what the test will be. But I do believe that you will be just fine. You are naturally strong and courageous, and that helps a lot. And I really do believe that the fact that you write those books goes a long way in helping as well. So, are you ready"? Gwennie took a deep breath and exhaled slowly, then said, "Like I told you. I'm as ready as I'm ever going to be, so let's do it".

They were now half a mile into the woods. Gwenie had been focusing on keeping her mind and mouth silent; focusing on the quiet. Shhe knew that if she wanted or needed to she could talk to Jim spirit to spirit, but she didn't want to do even that, fearing it might distract her from seeing or hearing something important. In fact, she was so focused that she couldn'teven sense Jim behind her in any way. She didn't hear him and neither did she sense his presence. Suddenly she caught slight movement to her right. She readied her walking stick for self-defense. Looking neither to the right or left, she kept her steady pace. Her heart was pounding a little and she had broken into a fine sweat, but she didn't really feel any fear. Twenty steps further and she found herself with a bear. It appeared to be a grizzly. It stood about six feet tall. For one split second Gwennie lost her focus. She thought, "A bear? Here"? But then she previous training kicked in. The bear's eyes were red, almost blood red. Still, she held her ground and said, "Through Jesus Christ I am more than a conqueror". She ran at the bear, jumped up and swung her walking stick with all her might and the bear disappeared. She suddenly heard clapping coming from behind her. It was Jim. "That was gret my Gwennie. I am so proud of you". And he meant that. He hadn't thought he could love her anymore than he already did, but when he saw her rin action, he knew he had been wrong. "For a second there I was a bit worried, but you snapped back in very quickly. You didn't llow the bear to completely break your focus". "Whew! Thnks Love. The bbear did throw me. I have never even heard of any bears around here, so that was a complete surprise". "That was the point of cjoosig bear. In battle, we ma encounter anything, especially since the enemy won't be able to hear us communicate with one another. This battle is a spiritual one, but eh enemy won't be above taking us out naturally. He wants to win this thing any way he can. If he can cause a heart attack or cause a us to fall nd crackou heads open; it's all the same to him and his crew". "Wow". So, are you the oe that sent th bear? How did you do that"? "No, I can't do anything like that. All I can tell you is that the "Might Warriors" do the testing. I'm not sure, but I think they are warring angels, but I don't know. Ll I know is that they are the ones testing you and I think somehow instilling into me all that I need to do in this whole thing". "Jim, what is this all about? Is this some "save the world" stuff, or what"? "Only in a sense. I promise you that I am not being cryptic. It's just that this is the obly answer I can give you at this time". He hoped she trusted him enough to accept that answer, and she had. After looking him in eh eyes for a few seconds, she said, "I believe you Jim. I know you are not oen to lie, so 'll just have to accept that answer". He hadn't realized that he had been holding his breath until she'd made that last comment. As he released it, he thought, "Lord, that was close". He hadn't lied to his Gwennie, he would never do that deliberately. Not to anyone, but especially not to the love of his life. But it had been revealed to him a short tiem ago that this battle was all about his Gwennie. It had something to do ith her being snatched out of those dreams. He didn't know all the details himself. But what he did kwo was that he was not at liberty to tell her the little he did know. However, id really did hurt him to feel like he was keeping secrets from the one woman he had fallen in love within his whole life. Of course, he had seen beautiful women over the years, but he had never tried to et close to one because of his shame of being a member of Goliath's family and later because of his size and age. But then he saw his Gwennie for the first time and knew he was in love with her right then. And ir had been that way since that day. She was the only person on earth that knew his real story and not th story he lived by. And she still accepted him nd loved him for himself, age and all. So, yes, it hurt to feel that he was keeping a secret from her, but he had to do as he was directed. And now that he knew that this was all about his Gwennie, he was even more determined to follow where and how he was led. He had to get this right for her sake. He looked at her beautiful face and saw that she was confused and a little tired. His heart seemed to melt in his chest. "So precious lady, are you ready to head back to the house now"? "Oh, are we done for today"? "Yes, we are. And youhave done so well, my Gwennie. I can't say it enough that I'm so proud of you". He reached for her hand, attempting to help her up but she sprang up with no help a all. He smiled and sid, "That's my Gwennie". She smiled then took his hand. They both looked at eh difference in their hand sizes, looked at each other and burst into laughter. When he coud speak, Jim said, "Like I sid, Mountain Man and China Doll", which brought more laughter.

Back in the house, they washed their hands and drank bottles of water. Gwennie saw that she had several phone messages, but she decided not to check them at that moment, peaying that nne of them were emergencies. She knew by the numers who the calls were from and had the feeling that all the callers only wanted to check on her, which she did appreciate. She didn't have very many friends, but the ones she had were really good ones and she loved them dearly. When she looked at her mantle clock, she saw it was after six o'clock. Knowing there was both pizza and salad left, she asked Jim if he would stay and have dinner with her. "If what's left isn't enough, I'll make something else to go with it". "Oh no, you don't need to do that. But we can always order another pizza or something if you want to". "Oh no, thanks. I was thinking of you. I'm hungry but not overly so. Come on, let get ready to eat".

Once Jim had left, Gwennie bgan to listen to her messages. The first was Delia calling to seeif she was okay. Ssame with Lynn. Both had left two messages, the last ones showing real concern for their friend. The last message was from Winnie. She too was calling to see if Gwennie was okay. Tears came to Gweni's eyes as she thought how god it felt to know that people cared about you. She wiped her eyes and began returning calls in the order she had received them.

Jim had decided to go to the shop afer leaving Gwennie. He wan't sure if he wanted to do some paperwork or get buy on one of the bikes that he personally was customizing. He looked at the clock and saw that it was almost eight o'clock, so he decided it was best to do the paperwork. He knew himself well enough to know that if he started working on the bike, he would lose all track of time. He wouldn't risk that because he needed to get some sleep because he had to be alerted to hear/feel what he was to do in Gwennie's preparation the next day. He knew it would be anything physical. But sometimes mental preparation could be just as tiring, especially if you weren't sed to it the way it had to be done. He started on the paperwork, thinking he would work until about ten. He should be home by ten thirty and in bed by eleven thirty. That would give him plenty of sleep, he hoped.

B the itme she finished returning calls, it was shortly after nine. Gwennie went into the kitchen to make sure it was neat again, then went in to tske a long hot shower. Once that was done, she crawled into her big comfortable bed and pulled the covers up to her chin. She hadn't realized just how tired she was until she was in the shower. She thought she'd better nt make it as long as she had intended, thinking she felt like she could lie down right under it and go to sleep right there. She started to say her prayers and fell asleep in the middle of it. It wasn't long before she was dreaming. This time she was in a strange room. Everything was gleamingly white. Someone was calling her name and that the same tie there was a strange pressing sensation on her chest, or was it in it? From there she ws suddenly back on the trail. She was on the stump, just looking and listening to the sounds of the woods. Suddenly, Jim appeared, but when she opened her mouth to say something to him, she was snatched away again. She awoke with a start, momentarily unsure of her location. Where was she? Fiinally she realized it was just a dream and that she was still in her bedroom and lying in her own bed. She laid there still for a fe minutes, then sat up. She began to speak out loud. "Okay. Something weird is happening here. The dreams are bad enough, but this sensation of being snatched out of them is something else entirely. What is really going on? Why am I being snatched away like that? And just who is doing the snatching? God, is that You? If it is, why doesn't it feel like You? A little bit more nd I would thik I 'm losing my mind. But I can't be, because Jim is in this with me. Lord, just what is this battle all abot? And why have I been chosen to take part in it? Why me? She begn t cry, feeling lost and alone. Why was this happening ot her? Why"?

Jim woke up snatching at the air. It hd been totally different this time. There was no battle, nor any preparation fr it. They were on the trail behind Gwennie's house. She had turned to say something to him and had been snatched away. This time he ahd tried to catch her but couldn't. Now he was wondering if that had been a test for him. And if so, hd he filed it? Was he not supposed to have tried to hold her there?

He knew the ensuing batte was about his Gwennie, but why? Was it about her life? Was it about her very soul? He truly didn't think I it could be about her sould, that woman loved the Lord with all her heart. No. This had to be about her life somehow. "Lord, if that was somkind of test and I failed, please forgive me amd give me the chance to make it right. I can't fail You or my Gwennie". Knowing it would be a while before he could get back to sleep, he got up and went int the kitchen to pt on a pot of coffee. Once he had his cup of his favorite beverage, he went into the den and sat in his recliner. He knew he didn't want the television on, but neither did he want to read. He just sat there, continuing to think, wonderin why Gwennie kept getting snathed out of their dreams? And why hd that only started happening when they wre in the dreams together? Was there something about him that was triggering that occurrence? Was there someone they didn't know about that thought tey needed ot protect her from him? All he knew for sure was that something was very wrong. The snatching away didn't feel like a part of her training, as he had initially thought. He felt strongly that there was someone else that was able to enter Gwennies's dreams, and if so, who? And why? And how could they just reach in and grab her like that without either of them seeing who it was? Or could it be what it was? It didn't feel like it was to hsrm her. It felt more like someone trin got protect her. But still, he would like to know for sure what it was all aout.

He finished his coffee, then decided he would read hs bible for a little while. He ran hs hand lovingly over it. Gwrnnie had given him that bible for Christmas fourteen years ago. That had beenthe first time anyone ahd ever given him a present of any kind since the death of Mr. Beardsley, the man that had given him his name nd taught him about the Lord. He remembered when Gwennie had presented him with the gift. It ws three days before Christmas. They had been friends for a little over a year by then. Gwennie had come to his shop with the package in her hands. "Merry Christmas my friend". He had felt she because he hadn't gotten her a gift. He had thougtht about it but had no idea of what she might like. And he had been embarrassed to ask Winnie for any gift ideas. When he hd asked sale women at a couple of stores, none of their suggestion seemed quite right for his very dear friend. "Wow, Gwennie. Thank you, but does this mean I don't get to see you on Christmas day"? "I'm afraid it does mean that. I'm spending Christmas with my parents down in Florida". "Oh, okay. Well, can I come see you before you leave". "As long as you can make it sometime tomorrow because I'm leaving on the day after". "You got it. I'll call to ee when is a good tiem to come by". "Sounds good, see you then". While they were talking, he noticed that she was wearing an exquisite bracelet, which gave him an idea of the gift he would give her for Christmas. After she'd left, he told his cre he would be back shortly and had gone to the nearest jewelry

BIG JIM

store, hopoing not to run into Gwennie. He had found a beautiful 24 karat gold bracelet with a strt shaped diamond in the middle of it. That wsit. He knew that was what he wanted her to have. He had it wrapped in eh store because he figured if he did it, it would only be disastrous. He thought that with his big hands he would have good intentions that would only go wrong.

The next morning, he had called Gwennie to see what would be th best time to bring her gift to her. They decided to have dinner together, so they would meet at six at Cracker Barrel. By the time Gwennie had arrived, Jim had been waiting for about fifteen minutes. When she arrived they were ushered to a table in a corner, which Jim was glad of. He planned to present Gwennie with her Christmas gift and he'd rather not have anyone too close around just in case she didn't like it. Once they were seated and had given their order, he presented her with the gift. She thanked him and asked if he wanted her to open it right then, to which he responded, "Yes, please. I nt to know if you like it". "Oh, I'm sure I will love it". She opened the gift and when she saw the exquisitely beautiful bracelet, she was speechless for a few seconds. Jim really didn't know what to think in that time. Did she like it? Dis she hate it? The silence seemed like an eternity to him. Finally, she spoke. "Jim, this is, wow, this is a really beautiful bracelet. I love it. But I'm sorry. I can't accept anything this expensive from you". She saw the hurt on his face and quickly said, "Let me explain, okay?

It's just that we don't know each other very well and well, we're not in a romantic relationship or anything ike that. And you can't convince me that this is not a very expensive piece of jewelry". "I thik I understand what you re saying. But may I tell you something? I was at a loss as to what to get you. In all my years, I hae never really shopped for anyone but myself. And I especially have never shopped for a lady before. I asked a couple of sales ladies to mke suggestions, but nothing they offered seemed good enough for you. But when I saw that bracelet, I just felt like that was you. I could picture it on your tiny little wrist". He stopped talking, looking for just he right words to say, without revealing too much of hwo he trul felt abot her. He sensed that if she knew, it would frighten her away from him. When he thought he had the right words, he said, "Gwennie, I relly do want you to have that bracelet, no matter the cost of it". He had to catch himself because he almost said, "I'd gladly give you even more, if I thought you would let me". Instead, he said, "There are no strings attached, okay? I'm not asking anything of you except that you keep being the beautiful, funny and true friend that you are to me. Please, accept it, okay"? His words had moved her heart in a way she, at that moment, didn't recognize. But she felt that it was somehow tight for her to accept his exquisite gift to her. "Okay, I do accept it, on one condition". "What''s that"? "Will you help me get it on? It's so delicate, and I don't want to brek it". "Gladly". Once the bracelet was on her wrist, he beamed, seeing that It; looked just the way he thought it would. He thought, "I was right. I was made just for her". Just as he finished putting her bracelet one her, the waitress came with their food and saw it. "Oh, that's a beautiful bracelet". Gwennie and Jim looked at one another and smiled. The waitress continued, "Looks iek you've got yourself a man who's in love". They both blushed and Jim thought, "I hope it's not that obvious to Gwennie. Not yet anyway. I just don't want to frighten her away". What Jim had never known was that Gwennie had paid closer attention to what the waitress had si than he had thought she did. That blush had been very real for her as well as for him.

That night, as Gwennnie did her packing for her trip to Florida, she couldn't help paying special attention to the bracelet. It fit her wrist just right and it really did feel like it belonged there. She thought about what the waitress ha said about Jim being in love. Gwennie admitted to herself that he was indeed a very special nd attentive friend, but she didn't think he was in love with her. She thought it was more that he didn't have very many friends and maybe was a little lonely. And as far as she knew, she really was his only female friend. Whether he was in love with her or not, he had choen an exquisite gift that had hardly left her wrist in the fourteen years sine he'd given it to her.

Jim shook his head to bring himself back to the present. He opened his bible and immediately found himself reading, Jeremiah 33:3, "Call to me and I will answer you, and will tell you great and hidden things you have not known". Jim read those two more times, then said, "Well Lord, I calling to You, because I sure fo need some answers. One in particular. I mean' You've revealed t o me that this whole battle thing is about Gwennie, so why is she now being snatched out of the dreams? And are You the One doing the snatching, or is there someone else involved that we don't know about? If so, how am I supposed towork with that? How am I supposed to prepare her for that"? He looked back down at the scripture one more time and said, "I sure hope you'll answer this oone. But if not, I'l just figure tht it's another eon of those things thT'S JUST onone of my business. Either way, I thank You Lord. I realy do".

Gwennie, seeing that she wouldn't get back to sleep, was sitting in front of her computer and was now working on her manuscript. Before too long, the storyline began to flow swiftly, which she loved. She hated sitting there wondering what to write. When the flow was smooth and swift, she could get lost in the world of her characters, and she loved being there. Not that she was mental or anything like that, she just really enjoyed writing. She loved being able to be creative and she loved even moe the way the Holy Spirit would speak wo her and guide her fingers ove reh keyboard. And she also felt a certain freedom when she was writing. Time didn't even seem to exist when she was writing.

Big Jim

It was nearly six in the morning when the creative juices slowed to a trickle. Gwennie stretched, shut off eh computer and got up to head to the shower. She knew she could try to get some sleep as she had nothing special to do, nowhere she needed to go. But she didn't want to risk having another dream. She ha done enough of that to last a lifetime. She got her clothes together, showered and dressed for the day and thought about walking the trail before breakfast. She looked at the clock and saw hat it was nearly tie for Jim to make his morning call and decided to wait until she had talked to him. She didn't have long to wait.

After their morning conversation, Jim was out his door and headed to his shop. Just as he straddled his bike, he had that now far too familiar feeling coursing through him. He knew he wouldn't be gong to his shop straight away but didn't know where he would end up. He eased out of his driveway, wanting to make sure in which direction he should go. He turned left and headed east. He's been on the road about twenty minutes when he was led to turn right onto a little country lane. About one hundred feet ahead he saw a car with its front end hanging down the car was slowly heading sown into a ravine. Inside the car was a young mother and her there smll children, one was an infant in its carsat. JTelling he mother that he was sent to help, Jim quickly found the right footing to im quickly lift the front end of the car and push it back onto the road. One of the children, a little boy of about five years old asked excitedly, "How did you do that? How did ou get that strong? Are you like "superman" or something"? Jim laughed and said, "Or something, my young friend". The young mother was rambling in her purse for a pen and paper so she could gt Jim's phone number so her husband could call and thank him. But when she looked back up, Jim was gone, bike and all, and they hadn't even heard him leave. Oh wow! I know we didn't dream this. He had to be an angel. There is no other way to explain it". Being too nervous to drive very far, the young mother thought it best that she and the kids went back home for a few minutes. She'd late for work and the children would ebe late for daycare and pre-school, but as jher mother had always said, "better late than never". Once they were all back in eh hose, she called her husband and told him all that had happened. When she had finished talking, they wee both quiet. Then suddenly her husband said, "Wait a minute. Some weeks ago, there was something on eh news about a really big guy catching a car in midair and setting it gently down. He's kept the car from crashing into a pole. I wonder if it could hav been the same angel. Either way, thank God that he was there at just the right time and that my family is safe". "Yes, I definitely agree".

By the time Jim go to his shop, his guys were already working. He thought he wouldn't trade his crew for anything in the world. They ahd all been with him for a few years and had al shown themselves

BIG JIM

to be loyal, honest and very hard workers. That's why he always did his best to mke sure they were paid and treated fairly. And apparently, they were satisfied employees, because they would tell others about their jobs, leading to other men wanting to come work at Him's Bike Shop. He hated turning them awy, but his guys were all he needed at that time. He walked in and spoke to everyone, thanked them for opening up and went into his office to call his Gwennie and share with her what had just happened. Not to boast or anything like that. It just always amazed him when the Lord use him that way. And what ws even more amazing to him was that none of the people he helped in that way never recognized him. As big as he was, surely they had seen him somewhere at some time, but they always behaved as though it was their first time seeing him. He loved that, because he just wasn't one who wanted to be in the "limelight". He had to leave a message asking Gwennie to call him back, as he wondered if she was okay. For soe reason he hoped she wasn't walking the trail, but rather was our somewhere shopping. Or maybe she was getting herself some good sleep. He doubted that last, but he could always hope. Oh well, she would call when she got his message. He hoped again she wasn't walking the trail. He knew he could speak to her spirit to spirit, but for some reason he didn't thik tha was the right thing to do at that time. He whispered, "Lord, just keep taking care of my Gwennie, okay"?

Gwennie was indeed out walking the trail. She had stopped and sat on her "trail seat", perhaps from habit. She had her walking stick lying across her lap sas she focused on the sounds of eh woods. She thought about speaking to Jim spirit to spirit, just for the practice, but decided against it. They had already talked, and she knew he would be deep into his work by that time anyway. She hadn't looked at eh clock before coming out of the house and she wasn't wearing a watch; only the brace;et that she had now worn for over fourteen yyears. She remembered the night Jim had given her that special gift and smiled. Suddenly, she heard a familiar voice softly calling her name. "Gwennie. Remember me, Gwennie"? Calvin. But Calvin had been dead for over twenty years. How could he e here. Her heart stated pounding. He was walking towards her, and she remembered the last time he had been close to her' the beating and kicking she had taken at his hands and feet. "Gennie, it's time we were together again. I won't hurt you. Not this time. I l-l-love you, Gwennie. Suddenly she remembered Jim saying that the enemy didn't care how he had to do it, he just wanted to stop them. Even if he had to cause a heart attack to make that happen. All she had been learning in her preparation for battle came flooding back to her memory. She now felt stronger, bolder. "Calvin was a devil alright, but you are not him. She looked the demon straight in the eyes and said, "I'm not going anywhere, but you are. Blessed be the Lord. He's my rock and He's teaching me to fight". With that last word, she swung the wwaqlking stick, aiming for the Calvin-demon's head. And when she hitit, the demon fell apart into smithereens. "Well, Daddy always said if you kill the hd, the body has to go". She hdn't realized how nervous she had become until she sat back down. She thought about the Calvin-demon trying to entice her to go with him. The only place he could hav been trying to take her was to hell. And that's one place she hd no intention of going to. Then she thought about Jim. Had he been tehe? Had he known about this? She thought now was as good a time as any to to speak with him. "Jim. Jim, are you there"? "I'm here, my Gwennie. You sound like something is wrong. What is it? Do I need ot oce to you"? "Jim were you here wth me just a few minutes ago"? "No, I wasn't. Why do you ask"? "I am on the trail, and something happened". He'd hoped she wasn't there alone. He's had a bad feeling. Nowhe wished he had been spirited to spirit with her nd felt bad for ot following his instinct. He sensed that she was crying. "Gwennie, I'm coming to you. Ot just spirit to spirit, but in person". He got up nd told his crew he hd to go back out, if he wasn't back close up shop for him. Without him saying it, they all knew it was soemtig to do wit his Gwennie.

By the time he arrived, Gwennie was back in her house. As soon as he walked through the door, she did something she had never done before. She collapsed against him and cried a loud sobbing cry. He picked her up and carried her over to the sofa and laid her there, then dropped to is knees to hold her hand and console her. When she had calmed down, he asked, "Gwennie, what happened out on the trail? It had to be bad to upset you like this". She grabbed a couple of tissues, wiped her face and blew her nose. "You relly weren't there with me? Yu really didn't see what happened"? "No to both questions. Now, please tell me what happened". As she told him about eh Calvin-demon, he had a sick feeling in the pit of his stomach. She thought it was a test, but it hadn't been. He didn't know everything, but he knew they would never do that to her. And this felt very wrong. The enemy really was trying to take hr out physically. "Jim, why ae you looking lik that? What are yo thinking"? "I'm sorry Gwennie, but at the moment I don't really know what I'm thinking, except this. I really don't believe that was a test. I think that was real, and it wasn't from anyone who loves you either". He thought about the times she hd been snatched out of the dreams. What in the world was going on? Is the Calvin-demon what someone was trying to sve her from? Or was someone or something helping the Calvin-demon? He had to find out the truth. Was her physical life hanging in the balance? He looked in his sweet Gwennie's face but didn't have the heart to tellher what he was thinking. What could he say and how could he say it? They both just sat qiet for a little while. Then, out of the blue, Gwennie asked, am I about to die? Is that why the Calvin-demon came for me"? Jim dropped his head, feeling ashamed that he didn't have the answer she was obviously expecting him to have. "Sweetheart, I don't have the answer t that. But I promise you this. We are in this thing together and we will find answers to our questions together. We will keep praying together, believing together and walking through thi thing together, hand in hand. As long as there is breth in my obody and I'm able to move and talk, I promise you that". Gwennie sat up and hugged him tightly. "I know that, Jim. I do", she said with her head on his shoulder. "I never thought I would be able to trust another Man. But I do trust you with my whole heart. And I know you won't let me go through this thing alone". She kissed his cheek, then his lips. "Thank you for being you. Thank you for loving me from your heart".

By the time Jim was comfortable with leaving his Gwennie alone, it was almost six o'clock. He had been with her for a little over five hours with thinking of nothing and no one but his lady love. He knew things were alright at the shop, no worry there. He had asked his Gwennie if she wanted him to go out and get he something for dinner, but she'd said she wasn't hungry. A part of him wanted to beg her to eat something, but he thought better of it. She semed to be drifting into a world all her own, and just for that time, he felt he needed to le her have that space and time. He just prayed that she wouldn't drift into a world where he couldn't get to her. They desperately needed to keep their lines of communication open, especially that spirit to spirit line. They still needed to prepare for the battle tat was coming. And now that he was sure that the battle was about his Gwennie, he was even more determined to fight with aqll is might and he would teach her in the same same fashion. He began to focus on the next day's lesson with her. A part of him felt it was time to bring out the "Swords of Truth", but a greater part told him it wasn't qite time for that. Besides, she was dangerous with her walking stick. She had quickly learned to use it in the name of the Lord and had conquered her enemies with ease. Her enemies. After her ordeal with the Calvin-demon there was no doubt that the enemy wanted to take her out completely. Jim knew that she loved the Lord with all her heart, and he knew that old slew foot knew that too. He knew that he couldn't just take her soul because she was kept by Jesus and was under the shadow of is wings. But had she been duped into going with that Calvin-demon, she would hve given her soul oer to the enemy, who was nobody but the devil. Jim had lived and learned enough to know that eh devil is always trying to draw believers of god over to his way of thinking and behaving. But Jim also knew that there were some people that the enemy worked even harder to separate from God and he knew now that Gwennie was one of those people. "Lord, continue to keep her, please. And tell me, show me, what I need to do for her as well".

BIG JIM

Gwennie never did eat dinner. She had lain on the sofa, trying not to think, for hours. When Jim had made his nightly cal to her, it had been hard to stir herself to answer. But knowing he would have been worried if she didn't answer, she did. "Hi Jim". "Hi Sweetheart. How are you"? He didn't like the way she was sounding and if it hadn't been so late, he would have gone right back ove to her house to be with her. "Oh, I'm okay. I have just been lying here trying not to even think about all that is going on. I mean, I know that we all have to die when our tiem comes. So, if I have to go down in this battle, I just want my soul to be right, you know"? "Don't even think that way"! For the first time ever, Jim had raised his voice to her and instantly regretted it. "I'm sorry Gwennie. I didn't mean to yell at you. Please forgive me. But I just can't let you give up. Not now, not ever. Look, this has been a lot for anyone to go through. The Calvin thing just shook you up, but that's all it did. Think about it. Even though you haen't completely gone through your training, you still got back on track defeted it. You are still strong, bold and courageous. I need you to remember that, okay"? Suddenly she was laughing, and he wondered about her and what was so funny. "I'm sorry my love. But that was some pep talk. But thank you. When you raised your voice, it shocked me back to reality, I think. It sounded like thunder. A big voice from a big man. That's a voice that definitely commands attention". They both laughed and he thought, "My Gwennie is back and I sure am glad". They talked for a few more minutes and when Jim was sure she was good, he said their nightly prayer and bade Gwennie good night.

Later, as she lay in her bed, Gwennie thought about Jim's booming voice when he had yelled at her. She hadn't been joking, it really had sounded like a clap of thunder. And she was glad for that "clap of thunder". It had brought her back to the task at hand. Apparently, this battle was even more important than she had initially thought. And it seemed that she was a vital part of it. She couldn't for the life of her figure out why. There was nothing that made her any more special than anyone else, so again, why had she been chosen for this thing? Could it be punishment for something she had unknowingly done? She would be the first to admit that he was nowhere near perfect; she made mistakes along the way. But she had always tried hard to do what was right. Her parents had always instilled that in her. Over the years they had reminded her that whatever we dish out will come back to us. Or in the words f her grandmother Essie, "Your chickens always come home to roost". And Gweni's father had periodically said, "The bible says that man born of woman is a few days and full of trouble. I sure don't want to add to that trouble". And as far as Gwennie knew, Franklin and Maddie Prowdler had both tried to live life doing their best to avoid adding to that trouble. And Gwennie had tried to follow in their footsteps and later, after receiving Jesus as her Lord and Savior, she tried hard to please her heavenly "Daddy". So, once again she wondered why she had been singled out for this battle? And why was Jim, who had seemed so confident suddenly appearing to be worried? What was the real truth about all of this? At some point she had finally fallen asleep and when he awakened the next morning, she found that she had slept quite soundly with no dreaming at all. Or at least n dreams that she could remember. She looked at the clock and saw that she had slept until seven twenty-seven. Through her window she saw that it was a dreary, rainy morning. "Oh well, no walking the trail this morning. Maybe later. She went into the bathroom to get herself ready for the day ahead, wondering what it held. As she showered, she prayed. "Lord, I sure do thank You for waking me up one more time. And I definitely thank You for letting me have some sleep without dreaming. And dear God, whatever You have for me to do today, please help me to et it right. But in case I do mess up along the way, I am asking in advance that You please forgive me, okay? And please keep on taking care of my big man. I know You have been keeping him all these years, but please keep on keeping him safe and blessing him". She then went on to pray for family, friends and ultimately, the world. By the time she finished praying, she was also finished getting dressed. She realized that she had broken routine. She usually like to thank God for waking her up while on he rknees. Later she would have her morning devotion while either sitting in her office or while walking the trial. But he felt that the good Lord wasn't holding that break from the norm against her. She went into the kitchen to figure out what she wanted for breakfast, while she waited for Jaim's good morning call. She knew she could call him, but he seemed yo like it better when he called her for the daily morning and night tiem calls. That didn't bother her though. What mattered was that he was faithful with those calls, those prayers, and that he was always there for her. Just then, th phone rang. "Good morning, my love. How are you"? "I'm fine, my darling. How are you"? It was Delia. "Oh Delia. I'm so sorry. I'm expecting...". Delia interrupted, "I know. You thought it ws your Jim". They both laughed, "Yes Delia. I thought it was him calling". "Well, I'm so sorry to disappoint you. But I'm calling to see if we can hve lunch together today? Think Jim can spare you for a little while to do that"? They chuckled and Gwennie said, "Oh, I think so. What time and where"? "How about Sammy's of Norwood, around one? I have the afternoon off, so I'd like to soak up the atmosphere over there. That sound good to you"? "Sounds good. It's been a little while sine I've been there". Having made their lunch plans, they said their "see you laters and got off the phone. Gwennie looked at the wall clock and saw that it was almost nine and Jim hadn't called. That most definitely was not like him. Concerned, she quickly dialed his home phone number but got no answer/ She then called his shop, but no one there had seen or heard from him. Now this was strange. Something was wrong. She grabbed hjer purse and drove as fast as she dared to get to Jim as quickly a she could. Once there she was a little relieved to see his bike and his truck were both in his garage. She rang his doorbell, then banged on his front door, with no response. Frantic, she ran around and banged on his back door and began calling his name.

Asleep in his recliner, Jim vaguely hard someone calling his name. He at first thought it was a part of the dream he was having, then slowly realized that it was his Gwennie calling him. "Gwennie? What's she doing here? Something Is wrong". He jumped up and with the speed only he could move with, was at the door in two seconds. "Gwennie, what's wrong"? He all but lifted her into the house. "What are you doing here? What's going on? Has something happened"? Wiping the tears from her eyes, she said, "I was scared that something had happened to you? "Why"? "Why? You're asking me why? It's well after nine". She looked at the clock nd said, "Well, almost ten now. You didn't call this morning, so I called you, but go no answer. So, I called the shop and they hadn't seen you or heard fro you either. So, I was afraid something was wrong, and I high tailed it over here to see about you". Jim, taking it all in, looked at the clock himself and saw that for the first tiem in years he had overslept. "Jim, you big goofball. If you're not sick or anything, why are you home now? You're always at the shop at this time of morning". He laughed at her calling him a big goofball. "And just what is so funny James Beardsley"? He began to laugh even harder, which was infuriating to Gwennie, who stood there looking at him with a scowl on her face. Finally, he said, "Gwennie, I'm so sorry Sweetheart. But you are calling me a good ball was just so funny to me. I know you're upset, so forgive me, alright"? "I guess". "Look, I just overslept is all. I didn't even hear the phone ring. I didn't think I would be going back to sleep earlier so I never even thought to set the alarm in the den. But let me call the shop. Come on into the den and sit down". After letting his crew know that al was well, he's just overslept, Mrk told him he's better let Ms. Gennie know that because she sounded fit to be ited. Jim laughed and said, "Too late for that warning. I found out firsthand. I'll see you guys in about an hour". He could only thank God for his crew. He could always count on them to keep things moving at the shop. Turning back to his Gwennie, Jim said, "Honey, I am really sorry that I scared you like that. Like I said, I overslept. I was reading my bible and fell asleep. I don't remember even feeling sleepy though. Anyway, I was dreaming about my childhood, baqck in the caves we lived inm and you were there. It was crazy. But for now, I have to get to the shop, so can we finih this later". "Sure. I'm meeting delia at Sammy's of Norwood at one. She has the afternoon off, so what may be a long lunch. But aqfter that I should e free. I assume we have a lesson thi evening"? "Yes, we

BIG JIM

do. And maybe my dream hd something to do with that, not sure yet. But anyway, I'll call you later", he said walking he rti the door. "I love you, my Gwennie". "And I love you my "Mountain Man". He kissed her forehead and out the door she went.

Delia was already waiting and seated when Gwennie arrived at the restaurant. "Well, hello Slow Poke. It's about time", Dekia said with a smile. "Hey Girl. I'm so sorry. For some reason traffic was just horrible. So, how are you"? "Girl I'm good. Just hungry as always". They ordered their beverages, then settled into their "girl talk". When the food arrived, Gwennie said grace and they resumed their conversation. Delia was telling Gwennie about the romantic relationship was in. "It looks like it may become a permanent situation". 'So, how do you feel about that"? Delia thought for a minute, then said, "Well, so far, he seems to be very honest, very consistent. He's very attentive. And I do feel like I'm falling in love with him. He has told me several times that he is in love with me, but just haven't been able to say those words to him. I've shared with him my reason for being so guarded, and he says he understands. Nd he really does seem to. I men, he's not trying to rush me into anything. And he just knows how to always be there for me. He sends me flower for no reason other than to say he loves me. So, if he continus the way he is, I think he's the one". "Aw, Delia, I'm so happy for you. I really do hope it all works out for he two of you". "Thanks, Gwennie. So,

195

how about you and Big Jim? When are the two of you going to just go ahead and admit that there is more between you than platonic friendship. It's easy to see that the two of you love each other". "Well, maybe that is a convesaation for another time". "Oh. Still in denial, huh? Oh, well, one day the two of you will give me the chance to say, "I told you so". "Gwennie, needing to change the subject asked, "So, how did you manage to get the whole afternoon off"? "Doctor's appointment. Got to have my annual physical. Want to go with me"? I guess I could. But I don't want to leave my car all the way out here though". "Well, why don't you leave it in the parking lot at work. It will be fine there. Want to do that"? "Sure", and that's what Gwennie did. And all afternoon they were two close friends having as much fun as two teenaged girls hanging out. Until Gwennie remembered that she and Jim would be having dinner and aother lesson later. Delia dropped her off to get her own car and Gwennie went home to plan dinner for herelf a Him. It would be something light and simple, yet heavy enough to handle a man sizzed appetite.

By the time Jim called, dinner was halfway ready. Gwennie had decided to broil whitefish and serve it with baked potatoes and a garden salad. She knew the fish would be a little light for an appetite like Jim's so she made ure she cooked twice the amount of what she normally would have cooked. She also baked two larege potatoes for him and made a larege bowl of salad. "There, she said to herself. "That should hold him for quite a while". She was putting the food on the table when he drove into her driveway.

"Cone on in, my big guy. How'd your day go after I left you". "Hello Sweetheart. It went well, thanks. How did your go, especially your lunch with Delia"? Gwennie laughed and said, "Well, there just may be a wedding in the future. The man she's been adating for about a year seems to be doing all the right things". Without realizing it, Jim flinched a little at that, and not without Gwenie noticing. "What was that about"? "What was what about"? "That little flinch thing you did. Why did you fo that"? Gwennie motioned for him to waqsh up and sit down to eat, which he did. "May I be completely honest with you, Gwennie"? "Of course, but I thought you always have been honest with me anyway". "Not about thsis". She looked at him in surprise. He continued, "It' not that I've deliberately lied to you or anything like that. It's just that since you have been in my life, marriage has been a rather sensitive subject for me. I'm sure you can guess why". "Jim, are you saying, are you saying what I think you are sayig"? Gwennie, since you came into my life, I have wondered so many times what it would be like to have you as my wife and to hve a family with you. Those are the times I've wished I was someone else. Someone, normal, I ggues I'd say. But with my true age and my size, I just knew that it could never be. I am happy for your friend, but I just wish it was you nd me talking marriage". He stopped and thought for a minute, then said, "I'm sorry. We aren't supposed to talk about thing slike this until the battle has been fought and won. Forgive me". Oh Jim. There' nothing to forgive. Honestly, I've wondered about being married to you. What any children would be l ike. It's true that I didn't know your real age. But Jim, it's you, your heart that captured my heart. Not your age or your size. I love you, my Mountain man". In one swift movement he lifted her from her chair and kissed her as he had never done before. "I love you so much, my Gwennie. There is nothing I would love more than having you as my beloved wife, but I guess for now I gues I'd better let you et dinner". They both laughed as he sat her back down in her chair.

After they'd finished eating, Jim helped her clean the kitchen, then they went into the den to talk and begin the next phase of her training. "Well, I didn't think to bring any kind of weihts with me, so I'm going to be your weights". Gwennie laughed hysterically, then said, "You expect me to life you"??? Nowit was his turn to laugh as he pictured her trying to life him. Finally, he said, No Sweetheart. We are going to arm wrestle". Gwennie held her arm up against his. "Really"? "Oh, yes. But don't worry, I am going to let you cheat". He sat down, cleared the end table and motioned for Gwennie to stand directly in front of him. Then he said, "Okay. You can stand and you can use both hands for now. I'm not going totake it easy on you, we can't afford that. So, you have to give it all you've got to take me down while using all you have learned about focus. But this time you will focus your ogysical strength, So now, let's go little lady. Try to mke me say "uncle", alright"? Gwennie put her tiny hand into his really large hand, which was a funny sight, but neither of them laughed. With their hnds in the proper position, he counted down from three to one, and the contest began. On the first round, he took her down instantly. "Okay, that was to be expected this time. Now, really concentrate on physical strength. Give focus to strength in your right arm at this moment. Now, try it again". They went a second round and this time Gwennie was able to hold him back fr a few seconds. "Good, my Gwennie. Now, you are getting it, so let's go again". It went on like that until they hd gne three rounds in which she hd been able to hold him back for no less than forty-five minutes. The had gone twenty-three rounds by the time he had said they were done for th night. Even though she hd been standing and had used both hands, Gwennie hd exerted so much energy that not only was her arm shaking, but her whole body was also. "Are you okay, my Gwennie"? "Am I okay? Am I okay? I just tried to arm wrestle a man that can lift cars and things. Twenty-three times, yet. And you ask am I okay"? They both began to laugh. "I'm okay, my love. But I just didn't realize that would be a whole-body workout. I mean I know that you are strong as an ox, if no stronger. But that was an abstract knowing. Today it became a concrete knowing. Mind if I ask a question"? "No, you know that. Ask anything you want". "Well, were all the men in your family excwptionally strong like you are"? "I don't know. Of coure, I know that my uncle goliath was exceptionally strong. My family used to tell how he once picked up the "stone of Samson" and held it up in the air. From there, they woudla rgue over who was stronger, Samson or Uncle Goliath. My grandmother said my father was a very strong man, tough not as strong as Goliath. Apparently, my father was a man of speed nd stealth, which made him a very good hunter". "Okay. So, his son has that speed and stealth, at least. I know I t must be hard to think of your faly, being the last one and all. I'm sorry if my curiosity nade you feel some kind of way". "Oh no, I do like to think of my family, well, mostly. It's just tht at three hundred and forty-seven years of age, it's getting harder and harder to remember. Sometimes I struggle to remember my given name, and most times, I can't anymore. You see, even back then, bos were seldom called by our names. Everyone was "Son:'. And the elders would point at eh one they wanted. I remember all of us boys would laugh at start pointing at one another and sat "you, Son". That usuallu got us in trouble, but not too badly. Actually, for the way thins were back then, life was pretty good in the caves. It was theoutside that brought us dangr. As I told you begfore, there were people that hated us because f ncle goliath. My family thinks that what happened to my father. They think he was out hunting and without thinking wondered out too far from our cave and townspeople ambushed him'. He stopped talking and shook his hed. "I do wish I could remember him, but I just can't. Still, I'm thankful for th things I can remember". "Wow. I can't begin to imagine what it must be like to be you. You truly are that "one of a kind guy", and you are all m mine". He smiled brightly, loving hearing his Gwennie cll him all hers.

When Jim left, it wa after ten thirty. He had told Gwennie, he thought maybe the next day could be a free one. She had been working hard and learning well; she had passed every test that she'd been given, and even one that the Warriors hdn't given her. As Gwennie debated whether to write or go to bed, wh thought about all the tests. The main one being the Calvin-demon. He was so insistent that she go with him, and she had a very good idea where he wanted he rto go. But she had no intention of going there. Not for Calvin, not for anybody. Not even Jim, if It were to come down to it. But anybody that knew Jim would ell you. He loved the Lord and went about doing all th good deeds he could, spreading the love of the Lord he loved. She thought, "Any demon would have a very hard time trying to use him in ay way to entice someone to hell. She turned her attention to her computer, deciding that she woud write for about an hour, which she did. But just before shutting it down, she looked at what she had written and found that she had typed the things she had continues to think about Ji, his life and their training sessions. "Oh no. How in the world did I manage to do that"? She deleted it all out and decided she'd best fo to bed. She just hoped she could sleep a sweet, deep, dreamless sleep. She was so tiredof dreams. She thought she'd had enough to last a lifetime. "Lord, ma I please have a night without dreams? I mean, a whole night. Please? I know Your I must be done, but I'm just making my petition known. Nevertheless, I love You and thank You". After her nightly preparations, she knewlt by her bed and began her nightly prayers. She didn't know how long she had been in prayer when she finally got up. Now she lay in her big comfortable bed, listening to see what God might have to say to her. Finally, she heard one word: "Rest", which she gladly did. It wasn't long before she was sound asleep. And soon she was on th trail behind her house. This time it was so cloudy that she expected rain to start falling at any moment. She had turned back, thinking she would wait to go for a walk. Suddenly, she heard the Calvin-demon talking ot her. "Come bak Gwennie. You hurt me really bad. I need you to come and see about me. You owe me that much". Then the voice changed into a wginy, almost screeching voice, as though desperate to have her attention. Dream Gwennie felt no fear, no compassion; she felt nothing but disdain for the entity. She turned and said with authority, Suddenly, Gwennie began to laugh, a loud hearty lqaugh. She then said,

"You don't get it devil. I dwell in the Secret Place, under the shadow of the Almght". As she spoke those words, she heard the unholy howl of the Calvin-demon as it hurried o escaper her presence. Gwennie turned back toward the house as she said, "Lord, thank You for saving me again". Just as she stepped into her house, starting t fall were the bigget drops of ain Gwenie had ever seen, even in real life. She looked up and said, and thank You for holding aback th rain until I was back in here. Thank You for loving me so much".

Him hadn't been able to get ot sleep for quite a couple of hours, but when he did fall asleep, it was a troubled one. He had begun to dream. Gwennie was on the trail, and she was in trouble. He tried his best to get to her, to speak to her spirit to spirit, but he couldn't make her hear him. He couldn't see her, couldn't see what she was up against. He began to audibly call out to her, but still with no results. He had yelled so loud that woke himself up. It took him a few minutes to realize that he wasn't on the trail, but in his bed. He sat up and tried to process that dream, wondering what it could possibly mean. In the beginning, he had pretty much understood the dreams, or the out of body experiences, if one preferred to call them that. But then, they took a strange turn. Now, the dreams seemed to target Gwennie while trying to have him excluded from them. And that wasn't food at all. He reasoned that for the tie being, he and she could still speak to one another spirit to spirit. But wha if some force was able to use the dreams to cut off their communication with one another? And does thi shave anything to do with his Gwennie being snatched out of the dreams? Is she being snatched out of the dream or is she being snatched away from him? And finally, how is he supposed to prepare gwennie for the upcoming battle? Jim was now sure that the battle was all about her, about he rlife.

Gwennie had only had one dream and had afterwards slept peacefully and soundly. When she awoke to the shrilling of her alarm, she stretched and thought, "wow. I slept good for the firt time in a few months. Thank You Father God". She went to the bathroom, then came back to kneel by her bed to properly thank God for keeping her safe throughout the night. She realized that her normal routine had been broken, and she wantd to get back on track. Then she wondered, "Do You want me "back on track, Lord"? For years, I hae been in the habit of doing my morning p[rayers and devotions one certain way. Maybe these dreams have served the purpose of msking mr vhsng things up a bit. Maybe God didn't want to feel like "just a hbit" to her or anyone else. Aybe He wanted her to change her approach, change the scenery nd maybe evenchange the time, since that change had taken place too. "Lord, I really do love You. If I m guilty of treating You like a habit, like something to do, please forgive me. And help me to honor You, to praise and worship You, to seve You in the ways that please You most.

In Jesus's name, please help me to get it right, Okay. Amen". She got up and got dressed, but didn't really want to start doing anything, as she was anticipating Jim's morning call and thought she could start work after that. She didn't have long to wait.

"Good morning, my love. How are you this fine morning"? Jim chuckled and responded, "I'm good Sweetheart, though from the sound of it, maybe not as good as you". Gwennie laughed and said, "Well, I o nly had one short dream last night. At least I think it was short. Anyway, I got some really good sleep. And this morning I feel more like the old Gwennie". "I'm glad to hear it my dear. Lisen, sinc we're not training today, why don't we go out for dinner this evening? Say around even"? "That sounds good to me. Where do you want to go"? "Now tha, my dear, is a surprise. You don't get to know until we are on our way there". "Oh, okay. I see. You want to kidnap me, huh"? "Yep. But you weren't supposed to know that, and you can't tell anybody". "And I can't even yell for help. Oh well. I guess I'll just have to be good with being kidnapped by you then. If it was anybody else, I'd have to show them what I'm working with now that I am being trained as a warrior". She laughed, but Jim didn't. "Okay, that was meant to ebe funny, but you ar not laughing. I know you, Jim. What's wrong"? "I'll tell you over dinner, Okay". "Oh no you don't, Jim Beardsley. It's been a while now sice we have been able to just relax and enjoy a dinner together. There is always something going on with us concerning this battle. Tonight, I would just like to enjoy being with you. I would like to just have fun together like we used to do, not so long ago". Jim's heart melted. He thought he just couldn't refuse his Gwennie that one request. "Okay my Gwennie. Well, I had a dream last night. You were on the path, and you were in danger. But I couldn't make you hear me, and I couldn't get to you. And with us seeing you snatched out of our dreams at least three times, I can't help wondering what it all means. Gwennie, I don't want to frighten you, but not everything you have been experiencing is from the Warriors and I have to be on my best gsame to protect you. But for some reason, I am afraid of doing just that. You once said that I always seem to know what to do. Well, that's not true, certainly not now. It's like we are losing control; like the Warriors are leaving us open to other testing they aren't in control of. And I don't know if this is how it has to be. Either way, I love you so much and I just don't want to fail you in any way". Tears were running down Gwennie's cheeks. "Jim, you will never fail me, at least not deliberately. But we both are old enough to know that sometimes thingshappen beyond our control. I know that you will always do all that is humanly possible to protect me, okay? I think we just have to follow through and play this thing out and see ow it goes. If I don't make it, it won't be your fault. Remember, there is only one God, and neither of us is Him. And His will is what shall be". Jim's heart was filled to overflow with so many emotions, love, admiration, pride for his Gwenne, and encouragement from her as well. He hadn't realized that a tear had rolled down his cheek as she talked. "Gwennie, just when I think I can't love you anymore, you find a way to make that very thing happen. My love for you is so deep that I can't find the roots of it. That may sound corny to you, but it's how I feel about you, my Gwennie". Now tears were freely flowing down her cheeks. She was so choked up, that she couldn't say anything. "Gwennie, are you okay"? Finally, she was able to speak. "Jim, that's not corny at all. It makes me love you even more as well. You are such a great and loving man, Jim. And the love you have for me makes me feel so special, so beautiful, so wanted and even needed at tiems. The way you love me only makes me love and appreciate you even more. And the more you give to me, the more I want to give back to you". "Thank you my Gwennie. That means more to me than I can ever tell you. But for now, I'd better pray and get to the shop". He began to pray a short prayer to cover them for the day and when he was done, they ended their call, and each went about starting their day.

Ted was outside when Jim drove up on his bike and parked in front of his shop. "Well, here the big man. How are you doing today"? "Hey Ted. I'm good. How are you"? "I'm good my friend. Just busy as usual, but thankful to have it that way". "I hear you. I'll probably be over later to get some of that good cooking". "Well Buddy, come on when you're ready. You know we'll fix you up real good". "I know yo will. I'd better get on in here before the think I've abandoned them". "Alright Jim. See you later".

When Ted got back into the café, Winnie asked, "Where in the world did you disappear to"? "Oh, I was outside talking with Big Jim. He was just getting in to work. He said he will probably be over for lunch. Anyway, did you need me for something"? Winnie laughed. "A little late now, don't you think"? Ted laughed too. "Well, I guess you got a point there". "Did Jim say anything about Gwennie and how she is doing"? At just that moment a swarm of customers came into the cafe, and they were too busy for further conversation about anything other than food orders. But now Ted also wondered about Gwennie, and if he ws okay. She hadn't been in the café for a few weeks and that wasn't like her. She usually showed up at least one a week, unless she wasin Florida visiting with her parents. He thought maybe he and/or Winnie would ask about her when Jim came in for lunch.

Lynn had called Gwennie just as she was settling down to write, and they had been on the phone for almost twenty minutes. It wasn't that Gwennie didn't want to talk to her sweet and dear friend. But she did want to catch up on her writing. "But Gwennie, you know how I gt tired of eating alone when my Harold is away. But this is my day off and I feel like cooking, so I don't want to go out to eat. With that being said, can I talk you into feeling sorry for me and coming over to have dinner with me"? "Oh Lynn, thanks for the invite, but I just can't. Mot tonight. Jim and I are foinf out to dinner". "Oh, okay. Well, one question then". "And that question is"? Gwennie was pretty sure she knew what it would be but wanted to give Lynn her chance to voice her curiosity. "My question is, are you and Jim any closer to admitting that you are more than "just friends"? I mean, neither of you is getting any younger, you know. And how you two feel seems to be so obvious to everyone but the two of you". It was all Gwennie could do to hold back the laughter. "Well Lynn, we re just happy with the way things are between us. Neither of us feels like we need to push anything, no matter how old we are or may be getting. Good enough answer for you Ms. Nosey"? They both laughed and Lnn responded, "I gues I'll have to accept it anyway". They talked a few more minutes, then got off the phone, promising to have lunch soon.

After speaking to his crew, Jim went straight to work on the vintage bike he had bveen working on for a few months. He still hadn't mde up his mind as to whether he would sell it or not, but he thought he was leaning more on the dside of keeping it for himself. He wondered how his Gwenie would like to ride this one; would she enjoy the ride ny bettr than she did on the bike she had ridden on with him. He kind of doubted it because bless her heart, he just didn't care a lot for bike or the biker world. She preferred cars, saying she felt safer in a car, there was at least something between her and another vehicle. He knew she had a point there. Thinking of his Gwennie made him think of heir earlier conversation and his heart seemed to flip and melt all at the same time. Oh, how he loved that little woman. But then he began to think about all the dreams and tests she'd had to endure quite successfully, he might add. But now, things were changing. He ddidn't know anymore what he needed to do or when to do it to help her prepare for the impending battle. He had figured out that someone, or something, didn't want her prepared for it. He knew that ultimately it was the evil that came to kill, steal and destroy. But he seemed to have an even stronger interest in stopping her in any way he could. Why? Could it be that old slew foot was afraid of her or some reason? Of course, Jim knew his own story and knew he wasn't who or what he appeared to be to the people around him; only his Gwennie now knew the whole truth about him. But now, he found himself wondering if Gwenie was who and what she appeare o be. He knew she was very honest, so he didn't wonder if she was deliberately being deceptive for any malicious reasons. Or maybe she just didn't know her true identity. He remembered one of the Warriors saying that she didn't know who she was and wondered how he had forgotten about that. But if she wasn't Gwennie, who was she really? And could her "loss of identity" be the key to the battle over her, even over her soul? But Jim was even more sure that she was snatched out of the dreams by someone who was very concerned for her safety. And he also felt very strongly that they weren't trying to protect her from him. Someone somewhere was just as afraid of losing her as he was of losing her himself. "Hey Jim! Where are you Man"? It was Mark, who had been trying to get his attention for a good five minutes. "What do you wan us to do about the throttle? When we tested it, it seemed to work fine, but now that it's one the bike it's not working properly, and we haven't been able to figure out what's wrong with it". Jim came bqack to reality and said, "What throttle"? "Man, are you okay? The throttle we have been telling you about for at least five minutes". "Oh. Sorry about that. Let me look at it". He stopped what he was doing and went over to see just what was gong on with the Suzuki Gixxer 150 Mark had been talking about. It only took two minutes for Jim to discover that the throttle cable hadn't been properly tightened. Mark laughed sheepishly and said, "Man, don't I feel stupid! I've been riding and working on bikes since I was sixteen, so I don't know why I didn't catch that. I'm sorry Jim". "Everybody is entitled to make a mistake once in a while, Mark. That's why e test these bikes so much before they leave this shop. Not on of us want to be the cause of someone getting hurt or killed on the road". He patted Mark's shoulder. You are good at what you do Mark, and you didn't stop until you found the problem and got it taken care of. That's what counts". Markk thanked Jim, who went back to work on his own project, his thoughts returning to his Gwenie.

Gwennie had been waiting for about an hour and was deep into her manuscript when she had a sensation that someone was watching her and had begun calling her name. This voice was faint, as though from another world. She sat still and quiet for a moment, then walked through her house to make sure she was still alone. She was very alert, wondering if this was yet another test. Finding nothing out of place abd all the doors and windows locked. She then mde sure her safety alarm was still armed and went back to her office to work on her manuscript some more. But no matter how hard she tried, she couldn't shake the feeling that someone wa watching her, very closely. She began to wonder if all the dreams had tests had begun to make her paranoid. She didn't kw a lot about paranoia, but she didn't think that was the case. This felt to real to her. Did paranoia feel as real as this felt to her? She realixzed she had lost the storyline flow, so she shut down her computer and got up from her desk, thinking maybe she would walk the trail for a little while. She changed into her hiking boots, grabbed her walking stick and started out her back door when she suddenly, loudly and clearly heard; "NO"! She had heard it so clearly that she expected to see someone, somewhere. But no one was there. She had even walked around her house outside, but all was still and q1uiet. All she saw and heard was ol Mr. Winston mowing his lawn and little Billy riding his tricycle in his yard. She knew neither of them had yelled anything at her. She went back inside, walked around inside her house again. And again, no one was there. So, was this yet another test she had to pass? Suddenly she felt so tired. She wished she could just let it all go. She went into her den, turned on her television, not caring what show or movie was on. She thought, "I am so tired", and drifted off to sleep. Then she felt like someone was shaking her, or rather jerking her. "Gwennie, you come back here. You can't leave us. Wake up! Please, wake up. Come back".

EPILOGUE

She opened her eyes and found herself in unfamiliar surroundings. Where was she? For that matter, who was she? She tri to move n couldn't. What in the world was going on here?

"Oh, thank God. She's awake", the strange woman standing over her bed said to someone. Then an older man appeared by her bed. They were strangers to her, yet they seemed so familiar to her. You're back with us, Baby Girl. You had us scared for a little while. That fever tried to take you away from us". "Fever"? "Yes, Baby Girl. You had a very jigh fever for quite quite a few days, almost a week". "So, I'm in a hospital thn"? "No Baby", the woman said. After the hurricane hit, the hospital, the part they can use, filled up very quickly. Thank God our house wasn't hurt any, so we brough you here to take care of you and Dr. Remo has come to check on you every chance he had to do so. Gwennie lay on the bed, trying to wrap her mind around what these two people were telling her.It didn't make any sense. It had to all be just another dream, a different kind of dream. She remembered working on her new bood, "Please Don't Pass the Sugar". Then she had started to go for a walk, when someone or something had yelled the work "No" to her. She had then gone into her den, turned on her television and laid down on her love seat for a nap. And now, here she was, so this could only be a dream. Oh well, she would son wake up. She had to, she and Jim had a dinner date t seven. She drifted off to sleep again and sometime later, the older woman came in the room to check on her. When she saw that Gwennie was awake, she asked, "Baby, are you hungry or thirsty? You haven' eaten in almost a week. And the only way we could get any fluids in you was by Dr. Rem starting an IV. You pulled that out twice, while quoting some scriptures. After the second time, we had to tie your hands down. We hated so much to do that to you Baby, but it was for your own good. So, again, are you hungry? Do yo think you can eat a little soup maybe"? Gwennie realized that she was a little bit hungry. "Yes, I think I could use something to eat". But first, please tell me who you are, and where Jim is. Is he here"? Who? Who is Jim"? 'You know. Big Jim. He is the only really big man in town. He owns Jim's Bike Shop. Next door to Ted and Winnie's Café". "Honey, I have no idea of who those people are. Are they new friend from up in Virginia"? "In Virginia? If I'm not at home, where am I? And who are you"? "Why Baby, I am your mother, and the man you saw is your father. And you came to Florida with us. This made no sense. It had to be another crazy dream. Gwennie knew that she was still in her house in Virginia. And Jim was the man she was in loe with and that sh new was in love with her, and they had a dinner date at seven. She looked for a clock and found one on the nightstand It wa now five forty-seven in the afternoon. It wouldn't be long before it would be seven and Jim would be there to pick her up. She tried to get up but had forgotten she had been strapped to the bed and that she had an IV in her arm. She thought, "Boy, this dream is really elaborate". She took a deep breath and didn't like what she smelled. Had she actually wet herself in her sleep? That wasn't like her. No matter how soundly she slept, she usually woke up to go to the bathroom.

When her mother returned with some chicken noodle soup nd crackers, Gwennie asked if she could please be untied so she could eat. "If you promise not to pull that IV out again, yes. I called Dr. Remo, and he will get here as soon as he can. I'll go get you a warm washcloth so you can clean your face and hands before you eat". When she returned, Gwennie said, "I really do need a good, hot shower". "Well, once the doctor sees you, we'll see about that hot shower. If he thinks you are too weak thogh, you'll have to take a "bed bath". "But that won't do. Jim will be here at seven and I won't be ready. And I certainly go out smelling like this". "Honey, again, who is this Jim you keep talking about? You have never mentioned meeting any man here that you were interested in, and certainly no Jim. "No, he's real", and she began to tell her mother, and now her father as well, about Jim, Ted, Winnie, Delia and Lynn. She began to tell them about how Jim was three hundred and forty-seven years old and was an indirect descendant of Goliath. She also told them some of the details of the tests she had been put through and dream she'd had. And when she started telling them about being snatched out of the dreams, her parents exchanged glances with worried looks on their faces. "Why are you two looking like that? I am telling you the truth". They both tried to calm her down, hoping to keep her that way at least until the doctor arrived. And when he did get thre, she tried to tell him what she had been trying to tell her parents. He listened patiently and then said, "Gwennie, for qyite a few days your temperature stayed up between one hundred and two and one hundred and four. We almost lost you four times because you stopped breathing and once your heart even stopped beating. That was no more than four hours ago. Patients have been known to have dreams, sometime quite bazaar ones while in the throes of high fevers. And I have seen them wake up, believing that the dreams ere real and that the real world was the false one. That's the case with you, my dear. And for a creative author like you, I'm really not surprised you had such vivid dreams. Now, we'll take that IV out, but I need you to drink lots of fluid, okay? You can get that shower and I'm sure you will feel much better. But you will still be weak for a few more days, so you will have to take it slow. And by the way, I hear that you are working on a new book. What's the name of it"? "Oh. It's "Please Don't Pass the Sugar". "Wow. That's quite an interesting title. Well, I think your parents can bring you into the office if you need me for anything. And don't worry, your full memory will return, and you will be able to distinguish between your dreams and reality. I'll see you all later".

Gwennie vaguely remembered that she had traveled to Florida to be with her parents for a couple of weeks. She had only been there for three days when they were being warned about a hurricane coming through. She remembered volunteering at the local shelter to help prepare for the storm, as well as heling her parents. She had known that she wasn't feeling very well but chalked it up to being tired. But now she was being told that she had been sick enough to have a high fever, and one that produced hallucinatioins yet.

After taking a long, hot shower and her mother had changed her bedding, Gwennie crawled up into it and sat up fr a while. Her mother brought eh rlaptop over to her and plugged it in for her. "I thought you might like to work on your new book while you rest". "I might, but I can't help wondering why Jim hasn't shown yo or at leat called". "Baby, everything will be alright", her mother sai as she kissed Gennie's forehead.

When her moter had gone out if the room, Gwennie rambled through her purse fr her address book. She couldn't remember Jim's phone number, so she hoped to find it so she could cll to seeif everything was okay. Finding the little book, she went straight to te "Js", but found no Jim listed. She thought maybe he hd listed hi name under the "Bs" but didn't fine him lised there either. She then looked under the "Ms", since she sometimes called him Mountain Man, but he wasn't listed there either. "Okay, I am not crazy. I mean, this whole thing is crazy, but I'm not. Why isn't Jim's phone number here? I need to call him to see if he is okay. And by now he is probably worried about me if he is okay". She laid her head back on the pillows and began to cry. Why is this happening to me"?

She finally booted up her laptop, thinking she would work on her new book for a while. But the problem was, she couldn't fine the manuscript. There was no "Please Don't Pass the Sugar" anywhere to be found. But what she idid see was a nanuscript titled "Big Jim". Curious, she began to read and as she did, she was quite shaken. The further over into the manuscript she read, the more shaken she became. Then, when he read where Jim had given Gwennie a 24k gold bracelet with a star shaped diamond in it, she jerked her left arm up and looked at eh bracelet she wore on it. She had fort noticed it when she was preparing to take her shower. She thought maybe one of her parents had put it on her wrist while he was sick. But how could hey have known to buy one like that? When her mother checked on her, she asked if one of them had bought it for her, but her mother said no. she said they had tried to remove it so it wouldn't get broken, but the clsp was so delicate, they thought they'd better just leave it on her wrist. Her mother said she's thought Gwennie had bought it and wanted to ask where she had gotten it. Once her mother had gone back out, Gwennie finished reading the manuscript, stopping only when she absolutely needed to.

And when he had finished reding it, she saw that the book cover had already been done. On the reddish-brown cover was the title: BIG JIM and at the bottom was her name: Gwendolyn "G.C". Carter. She thought, 'then apparently, it's true. I REALLY was dreaming. I was dreaming about the book I had written". She looked at the exquisite bracelet again and said, "But if it true that I was dreaming the book, and Jim is just a character in that book, why is this bracelet real and where did it come from"?

www.ingramcontent.com/pod-product-compliance
Lightning Source LLC
LaVergne TN
LVHW091530070526
838199LV00001B/4